'I understand [...] the summers.'

Puzzled by his new tack, Jenny answered warily, 'Yes, I did.'

'And didn't you go to pharmacy school?'

The direction of Noah's line of questioning became clear and she went on the offensive. 'I'm sure you're aware of my degree, so why are you asking?'

'Doesn't your education mean you're qualified to step into your uncle's shoes?'

Her reply stuck in her throat and she studied the ceiling until she could choke out the words. 'It does, but I won't.'

'Why not?'

She hesitated, hating to tell Noah what she hadn't been able to tell her uncle. 'Because I'm not a pharmacist any more.'

**Jessica Matthews'** interest in medicine began at a young age, and she nourished it with medical stories and hospital-based television programmes. After a stint as a teenage candy-striper, she pursued a career as a clinical laboratory scientist. When not writing or on duty she fills her day with countless family and school-related activities. Jessica lives in the central United States with her husband, daughter and son.

**Recent titles by the same author:**

HIS MADE-TO-ORDER BRIDE

# PRESCRIPTIONS AND PROMISES

BY
JESSICA MATTHEWS

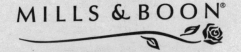

DEDICATION

In loving memory of my grandmother, Helen. 1901-1999

ACKNOWLEDGEMENT

Special thanks to Kathleen Nance, Pharm.D. for sharing
her expertise. Any errors are my own.

First published in Great Britain 2000
Harlequin Mills & Boon Limited,
Eton House, 18-24 Paradise Road, Richmond, Surrey TW9 1SR

© Jessica Matthews 2000

ISBN 0 263 82255 9

Set in Times Roman 10½ on 12 pt.
03-0008-49417

Printed and bound in Spain
by Litografía Rosés, S.A., Barcelona

# CHAPTER ONE

'You can't do this.'

The deep male voice diverted Jenny Ruscoe's attention from the pharmacy's storefront window. She shielded her eyes against the early afternoon sun's rays to stare at the man who'd arrived unnoticed.

Although he wore designer sunglasses, she'd have recognized Dr Noah Kimball anywhere. He cut a fine figure with his tall, athletic build, short hair the color of freshly brewed Colombian coffee and a face on par with any male model's.

Glancing over his shoulder, she saw a late-model, dark blue Blazer parked at the curb. She must have been totally lost in her thoughts if she hadn't heard his approach.

'I can. I have,' she replied. Several people had already stopped to talk about the sign she'd placed in the window. While their responses had ranged from the politely curious to deeply disappointed, no one had been as openly hostile as Noah Kimball.

She shouldn't have expected otherwise. From the moment she'd stepped foot in the Hays hospital where her uncle had been transferred after his collision with a loaded cattle truck, Noah Kimball had given her a chilly reception, an it's-about-time-you-got-here comment and an admonition not to upset his patient.

As if she'd dropped everything to fly from Grand Junction and agitate her uncle while his grip on life faded.

The only time Noah had showed a different facet to his character had happened right after the blips on Uncle

5

Earl's heart monitor had tapered to a flat line. She'd turned to Noah without thinking and had found solace in the shelter of his arms. His shoulders had trembled under her hands as he'd struggled with his own emotions. Later, after they'd pulled themselves together, she'd seen his red-rimmed eyes as he'd offered her his handkerchief.

After that evening, an invisible barrier had formed between them as if those moments had never happened. Since the funeral, he'd treated her like a stranger and she'd been too caught up in settling Earl's affairs to care.

Knowing of his loyalty to her uncle, she'd expected him to protest her decision. However, she hadn't expected this strong a reaction to her poster's message.

GOING OUT OF BUSINESS.

He motioned to the window. 'How can you wipe out fifty years of service to this community? Do you realize what the repercussions will be?'

'Yes, I do, but I'm surprised you heard the news so quickly. I only hung the notice this morning.'

'Naturally the news travelled fast. This isn't a restaurant where, if it closes, three others are standing by to fill the void. Ruscoe Pharmacy is part of Springwater's history. Did you expect to drop your bombshell and slink out of town without hearing a public outcry?'

'I'd thought of shooting fireworks and hiring a brass band to observe the occasion,' she retorted, 'but the band director is on vacation and fireworks are banned in the city limits until the Fourth of July.'

Although Jenny didn't consider herself a sentimental person, her family's contributions to the town deserved some sort of commemorative fanfare. A neatly lettered poster didn't seem a fitting end to the era.

He folded his arms across his chest. 'Your earth-shattering announcement caught the town by surprise, so

I presume you're either an expert fraud or you decided this on a whim.'

His mirrored lenses hid his eyes, but she imagined his gaze being as piercingly cold as his tone. She gritted her teeth at his close-minded attitude.

'I'm not impulsive and I never set out to deceive anyone. Everything came to head and I had to do something. This…' she motioned to her window '…was my best option.'

The battle for the drug store's survival had started a month ago, on the very day the lawyer read her uncle's will. She'd intended to maintain the status quo until she'd found a suitable buyer, but her alternatives had become fewer and fewer until her best-laid plans had come crashing down. Literally, overnight.

Noah Kimball would never know how much she'd agonized over her decision. Losing the man she'd looked upon as her father, that had been bad enough. Now she shouldered the pain of seeing his legacy disappear into the annals of history.

'Well, if you're waiting for the city council to name a park after you, you can forget it.'

'I'm not interested in your popularity contest. I carefully weighed all the facts and came to the most logical conclusion.'

'Do tell.'

A bead of perspiration trickled down the side of her face. In spite of being bare-legged and wearing a sleeveless green-and-red plaid cotton shirt and khaki skirt, she felt hot enough to melt into a puddle. She took a perverse pleasure in imagining how much more uncomfortable he had to be in his dress clothes.

Out of the corner of one eye, she saw several nearby business owners step outside their establishments and begin sweeping off their already-clean sidewalks. Clearly, they didn't want to miss a single scene of the action taking place under their noses.

Jenny, however, wasn't in the mood for an audience. 'We don't need to discuss this—'

'Yes, we do.'

She continued as if he hadn't interrupted, well aware of the growing group of spectators. 'In the heat. Believe it or not, the air-conditioning is working.'

Her uncle had replaced the heating and cooling system last year and it was one of the few things in the old building that functioned properly. With any luck, a cooler environment would also lower Dr Kimball's rising temper.

'Fine.' He waved his arm toward the door. 'After you.'

The bell above the door jangled as she regally limped inside, thanks to the blister on her right heel. The familiar blend of scents, consisting of everything from cherry syrup to peppermint, surrounded her like a hug from an old friend. In spite of the comforting aroma, she could pick out Noah's special fragrance—the combination of soap and healthy male which she remembered so vividly from the evening spent in Uncle Earl's ICU room. Normally, she would have been allowed fifteen minutes every other hour, but none of the nurses had dared to enforce their rules, with Noah hovering nearby.

The air cooled her sun-warmed skin but did nothing for her dry throat. Before she could courteously offer a glass of iced tea, he'd replaced his sunglasses with a pair of oval wire-rimmed frames and had headed over to the corner where a large, insulated sports Thermos stood on a rickety table. Depending on the season, Earl had always kept a free pot of coffee or iced tea available for his customers, and she'd observed the same custom.

As he filled the cups from the spigot, the play of muscles across his shoulders drew her attention. His athletic build filled out his moss-green shirt and dark trousers in all the right places. Her uncle had once told her how Noah played a mean game of one-on-one basketball, and she could easily picture him on the court, wearing shorts and a tank top. Underneath his professional attire, he obviously had powerful legs, a washboard stomach, and long, strong arms.

The top button was undone and revealed smooth skin in the hollow of his throat. She was almost surprised that he didn't wear a tie, but either he preferred a more casual appearance or chose not to suffer one in the heat.

Noah's garments were of good quality name brands, but not ostentatious. Considering how Springwater was a town of low- to moderate-income families, he'd clearly purchased those items that wouldn't flaunt his social status or his physician's income.

At five feet ten, she often looked down on people, or at least met their gazes head on. However, he had a five-inch advantage which under the circumstances, gave him a psychological edge in the battle about to begin. For that reason alone, she hoped he would sit so they could air their differences on an equal footing.

He turned toward her and she studied his features. His high forehead, straight nose, and well-defined cheek-bones obviously came from a gene pool of handsome men. Although she didn't expect to see a smile, one would certainly have added to his masculine charm.

She accepted the paper cup he held out to her. Considering the situation, it seemed incongruous to be on the receiving end of his courtesy. Once Noah Kimball broached the subject he'd come to discuss, he would show her no mercy.

Deciding to make herself physically comfortable in an

emotionally uncomfortable situation, she hobbled toward the three chairs standing against the north wall where customers could wait for their prescriptions if they were so inclined. 'Would you like to sit—?'

'What's the matter with your foot?' A wrinkle of curiosity appeared on his forehead as he studied her.

'Nothing, really. Just a blister.' No doubt she'd earn a scathing remark if he knew she'd gone on a walking tour of Springwater last night without changing from sandals to her tennis shoes.

'Do you have something to put on it?'

'We're standing in a drug store. I'd say so,' she said dryly.

'But *did* you?' he persisted, his brown eyes intent on her face.

'A Band-Aid. Satisfied?'

Noah rolled his eyes in a heaven-help-me look before he turned toward the aisles of over-the-counter medications.

She thought about waiting to sit until he did, provided he finally chose to do so, but the dull pain on her heel reminded her of how badly she wanted to remove the shoes responsible for her predicament. She sat and slid her foot out of the sandal far enough so the back strap didn't rub on her sore spot.

Noah's voice carried from across the room. 'Did you, or did you not, promise Earl on his deathbed that you'd keep his business open?'

She flinched under his reminder. Since Noah had been with her at the time and had witnessed their short conversation, she couldn't deny it. 'Yes, but—'

'I'd like to know why you're not living up to your commitment.'

'I told Uncle Earl that I'd keep things running while he recovered,' she corrected. 'He didn't.'

'Getting technical, are we?'

His tone rankled, but she choked back a reply and counted to ten. 'No, just pointing out the facts.'

'I warned you from the moment you stepped foot in the hospital not to hope or plan for his recovery. His injuries were too extensive. Earl was asking for more than your temporary help and you know it.'

She leaned back in the chair and bit her lip as the truth stung. Guilt-ridden over the events of the past year, she'd have promised her uncle anything. Anything at all. Those, however, were circumstances that she didn't intend to explain to the overbearing Noah Kimball.

'I was well aware what my uncle was asking of me.'

'I also told you of Earl's worries about the store. Did you think you could promise a dying man anything in order to ease his last moments?'

She bristled under his accusation. 'I fully intended to honor every word I said.'

He arched an eyebrow at her as he paused in his search. 'Then what changed your mind?'

'Would you like a list?' she asked with sarcasm.

'In a word? Yes.'

His attitude pressed a sore spot on her pride. 'I'm not under any obligation to tell you a thing.'

'No,' he said, 'but as a close friend of Earl's, as a witness to your promise, and as a physician who sends a lot of business in your direction, I'm entitled to some sort of explanation.'

She started to refuse, then reconsidered. She had nothing to lose one way or the other. In fact, Noah might shed some light on the questions that had arisen.

'The problems facing the pharmacy were—are—overwhelming,' she began. 'I'd barely recovered from one disaster before another one hit. I went into crisis management mode and couldn't get out.'

'So you're quitting, just like that.' He snapped his fingers.

'No, it's not "just like that."' She mimicked his gesture. 'As I said before, I fully intended for Ruscoe Pharmacy to carry on. After all, it's been in my family for two generations. I don't want to see the business fold any more than you do.'

'Actions speak louder than words.'

'Do you want to hear this, or not?' she ground out.

He frowned, but fell silent, gesturing impatiently in a go-ahead motion.

Jenny drew a bracing breath. 'After studying Uncle Earl's books for the past month, I found he—the pharmacy—was in trouble. He's shown a steady loss in recent years—'

'That's impossible. He had the corner on the market in this town.'

'Maybe so, but how long could *you* stay in business if the amounts in your accounts receivable exceed the bottom line in your accounts payable?'

His expression became thoughtful. 'Your uncle was a generous man.'

'I know he was.' He'd helped her meet her own expenses during college when she'd run short of funds. 'But his generosity contributed to his problems.'

Noah started to speak, but Jenny forestalled him with a raised hand. 'I'm simply telling you what I've found. John Grant is the accountant. He can confirm everything I've said.'

'Earl never, *ever,* mentioned having financial difficulties.'

'I'm sure he didn't,' she said, aware of just how close-lipped her uncle had been, 'but the signs are all here and probably have been for some time.' She waved her arms in an all-encompassing motion. 'Does this look like a successful, up-to-date, profit-making operation?'

She drew his attention to the most conspicuous flaws. 'See the brown patches of old water stains on the ceiling? Don't forget the one left behind from last week's storm. By the way, did you notice that the awning outside was missing?'

Warming to the subject, she continued. 'The wallpaper's peeling. The display shelves are falling apart. Someone's taped the torn vinyl seat cushions with gray duct tape to hold in the stuffing. Oh, and don't forget the table in the corner. There's an inch-thick pad of cardboard underneath a leg to keep the whole thing level.

'And in case you hadn't noticed, in some places, the floor tile has been worn completely through. Why, even the design is gone. It used to be brick red with gold and black flecks instead of this faded reddish-pink color. I know, because I helped pick it out twenty years ago.'

As a twelve-year-old, she'd been thrilled and overwhelmed with the responsibility. Hoping to please her uncle, she'd spent days weighing the pros and cons of various colors and patterns. She'd even polled several business owners for their opinions of which brand held up the longest before she'd presented her final choice to him for his approval. Her aunt had argued in favor of something else, but Earl had stood by her recommendation, claiming it was exactly what he wanted.

Eunice had ruled the roost at home, but in matters concerning his pharmacy only Earl exercised authority. He'd maintained complete control of his professional world.

Noah turned down another aisle. 'Things are run-down,

but a good carpenter can work wonders with a few nails and a gallon of paint.'

How could the man be so obtuse? If that was his attitude, she wondered how he maintained his own office building.

'A few nails and a fresh coat of paint won't scrape the surface of what's needed,' she stated firmly. 'The electrical system is an accident waiting to happen. I doubt if it's been updated since Ike ran for office. When I plugged the coffee-pot in this morning, sparks flew. I can't imagine what would happen if I plugged in my laptop.'

'OK, I'll concede the wiring is bad. What's next on your infamous list?' He hesitated, then changed the subject. 'Hey, where's the antibiotic ointment?'

She gritted her teeth. 'For your info, Dr Great-Idea, you've discovered the next major problem. The inventory.'

Standing a head above the top shelves, he frowned at her. 'I dropped by not too long ago. I saw plenty of merchandise.'

'Oh, we were stocked all right. Unfortunately, most of the products were outdated. I had to throw out nearly everything, including the ointment you're looking for. Just this morning, I found a bottle of aspirin that should be displayed in a museum.'

Suspecting his response would be to 'order more', she continued. 'From the way this place looks, an unsuspecting person could easily think he'd wandered into someone's attic or a flea market, not a drug store.'

She rose and hobbled to the front where she plucked a Sorry board game off a bowed shelf and blew the dust off the lid. 'See what I mean?'

Not allowing him time for rebuttal, she pointed to a row of stuffed animals. 'The poor teddy bears aren't brown any more. They're a dingy shade of gray.' She patted one bear's back and a dusty cloud drifted upwards.

'So Earl's attempt to diversify with a gift shop wasn't a marketing success. Try something else.'

She took a few steps and leaned against the counter bearing an antique cash register, frustrated by her unsuccessful attempts to make him study his surroundings with her realistic eye.

'Even if the building was in top form and the inventory was all brand new, I still don't have any manpower.'

'Yeah, let's talk about your lack of manpower,' he said with obvious disdain as he skirted the racks to stand within arm's reach. 'I may not have a business degree, but even I can see that if you need a labor force, you shouldn't fire your only employee.'

In Jenny's experience as a pharmacist, being on the receiving end of a physician's vitriolic tongue was nothing new. She'd run into doctors like him before, men—and a few women—who wielded their authority with a heavy hand and on a regular basis. This time, however, she could voice her feelings without the fear of a reprimand from her superiors.

'For your info, Herb Kravitz resigned.'

'Forced into it, most likely. Wasn't he dusting properly?'

'Don't be ridiculous,' she snapped, stiffening her spine at his sarcasm. 'The rumors are wrong. Herb wasn't forced out of his job. Why would I purposely let him go when I needed him?'

He shrugged. 'Who knows? Out with the old, in with the new? Or maybe if he quit, you won't have to dig in your pocket and shell out severance pay.'

A bitter taste filled her mouth. 'You're bound and determined to think the worst of me, aren't you?'

'Just calling it like I see it.'

'Then take my advice, *Dr* Kimball. Get your eyes examined. I don't like the position I'm in any more than you do, but Herb refused to follow my suggestions for operating more cost-effectively. He was very unhappy about taking orders from a woman, especially one who's younger, so he left.'

Herb Kravitz had asked for a raise yesterday and, after hearing her refusal, he'd voiced his unflattering sentiments in the most blunt terms possible. He'd expected a portion of the business in exchange for the sweat he'd poured into the place and had been sorely disappointed.

He'd balked at seeing a novice enjoy the fruits of his labors. Rather than work like a plough horse for her and her tight-fisted aunt, he'd decided to cut his losses and leave while he was young enough to do so. At forty-eight, he shouldn't have trouble finding a job where he'd be appreciated and well rewarded. Or so he'd said.

According to the records, her uncle had compensated the portly fellow well, paying Herb a more handsome salary than he'd paid himself. Having just seen the estimates for the most pressing building repairs, and knowing that her aunt had wanted to *cut* his wages, not increase them, Jenny's options had been—and still were—limited.

'Then hire another pharmacist,' Noah remarked. 'One who doesn't have a problem with a female being the boss.'

She struck a thoughtful pose. 'Well, gee whiz. Now why didn't I think of that?' Then, in her normal tone, she added, 'I've looked for a pharmacist, but haven't found anyone interested. In the meantime, promise or not, no pharmacist means no pharmacy.'

'What about a locum?'

Jenny shook her head. 'No luck there either. Uncle Earl

had a hard time finding a replacement when he took a rare but well-deserved vacation. Most aren't willing to come to the plains of Springwater unless they receive an extremely lucrative incentive. That's how he hired Herb in the first place.'

The silence seemed to last a lifetime as Noah's piercing gaze rested upon her.

'What do you expect the people of this town to do?' he finally asked in a clipped voice. 'We have a lot of elderly people who, for one reason or another, can't hop in a car and travel thirty minutes one way to fill their scripts.'

'I know it will be a hardship. When I get back to Grand Junction, I'm going to find someone who'll want to establish a pharmacy here. That's the best I can do.' She cleared her throat to hide the husky quality of her voice. 'For what it's worth, my decision didn't come easy.'

'Your "best" isn't good enough.'

Jenny refused to show how much his accusation hurt. 'You don't play fair, do you, Dr Kimball?'

He stepped closer. 'I'll tell you what's not fair. It's not fair for old Mr Samuels, who's blind from diabetes, to figure out how he'll purchase his insulin. Try to explain to Betty Lancaster, who hasn't driven in twenty years and has no family in the area, how fair it will be for her.'

'I know it will be inconvenient—'

He scoffed. 'Inconvenience is when you're in a hurry and have to run across town for something you forgot. "Inconvenient" doesn't even *begin* to describe the problems people will face.'

Her anger rose to match his. 'I'm sure this will only be temporary.'

He folded his arms, his feet planted apart in a warrior's stance. 'And what if it's not?'

She didn't answer, unwilling to consider the possibility. If only she'd known of Earl's troubles before now. But she hadn't and now she had to deal with the situation as best she could.

Jenny hadn't realized she'd spoken aloud until Noah asked, 'Would it have made a difference to you?'

His accusatory tone raised her hackles. 'Yes.' In spite of her reluctance to involve her uncle in her personal problems of a year ago, if she'd known how much he'd needed her, she would have considered other alternatives, made other choices.

They'd both apparently suffered from an over-abundance of pride.

Whatever Earl's excuse for being so close-lipped about his problems, shame had prevented her from divulging her tale. He'd done so much for her over the years, and she'd hated to admit her failures. Nor had she wanted him to see how badly her professional self-confidence had eroded.

Unfortunately, the same stubborn pride that had carried her through school had cost her dearly. She'd lost precious time with her uncle, not to mention the opportunity to salvage his beloved pharmacy from ruin. If she'd returned twelve months ago, perhaps this particular chapter of her history would have had a different ending.

'I understand you worked here in the summers.'

Puzzled by his new tack, Jenny answered warily, 'Yes, I did.'

'And didn't you go to pharmacy school?'

The direction of his line of questioning became clear and she went on the offensive. 'I'm sure you're aware of my degree, so why are you asking?'

'Doesn't your education mean you're qualified to step into your uncle's shoes? Or Herb's, for that matter?'

Her reply stuck in her throat and she studied a brown patch on the ceiling until she could choke out the words. 'It does, but I won't.'

'Why not?'

She hesitated, hating to tell Noah what she hadn't been able to tell her uncle. 'Because I'm not a pharmacist any more.'

# CHAPTER TWO

IF NOT for the tense atmosphere, the shock on Noah's face would have been humorous. Jenny had startled him with her explanation and she doubted if he was often surprised to the point of being speechless.

'What do you mean, you're not a pharmacist any more?' he asked. 'Did you lose your license?'

'No,' she said quietly. She'd changed professions before her life had come to such an unthinkable situation. 'I've been teaching school for the past year. Chemistry.'

'What happened?'

Jenny wasn't ready to go into detail. Hard-as-nails Noah Kimball wouldn't have understood, especially since he went out of his way to think the worst where she was concerned. He clearly saw life in terms of black and white, good and bad, right and wrong. Little, if anything, fell in between.

'The stress became more than I could handle, so I resigned,' she said, speaking nonchalantly of the period in her life which had been so traumatic. 'I have my teaching degree, so when I heard of an opening at one of the high schools I jumped at the opportunity.'

'Did Earl know about your career change?'

She studied her sandals as she shook her head.

'So you quit coming back to Springwater.'

'My visits dropped off months beforehand,' she corrected him. 'I worked six and seven days a week at the hospital and couldn't get away long enough to make the

20

trip. After I changed gears…' she hesitated '…I couldn't bring myself to face him.'

'Earl took great pride in your accomplishments, but he missed you. He wanted more than phone calls and letters.'

'Don't you think I know that?' she burst out. 'Right or wrong, I did what I thought was best at the time and I have to live with my decision.'

Noah didn't need to know how much she regretted hiding her new life from her uncle. She'd finally decided to tell him this summer, but if she'd known he wouldn't live much longer she wouldn't have waited… He'd always been so healthy and such a conscientious driver. She'd never dreamed he'd be the victim of a car accident while still in his prime.

'And now you're making a decision that everyone else has to live with as well.'

His tone rankled her and she lifted her chin. 'Yes, they do, but it can't be helped.'

He shook his head. 'Lady, I don't know about you, but I think it would be a lot more stressful to deal with today's teenagers than counting out pills.'

'Obviously you haven't worked with overbearing physicians like I have,' she said sweetly, hoping he understood that she counted him in the group just described.

He cocked his head and gave her a salute. '*Touché*, Miss Ruscoe.'

'In any case, because Herb has resigned, I can't run things myself.'

His eyes narrowed. 'Why not? Herb did.'

'I can't be *here* to run things,' she corrected. 'I have other commitments.'

'I thought one of the perks to teaching was the opportunity to loaf away the summer months.'

Her mouth curled with disgust at his misguided view.

'We loaf when we're not taking classes, teaching summer school, working on school committees and special projects, or getting ready for the next school year. As for myself, my responsibilities for the next two months are personal, not professional.'

'Are they more important than helping an entire community?'

Jenny thought of her friend, Susan Fenton, and her daughter, Carrie. 'Equally as important,' she said.

'Haven't you heard of the saying, 'The good of the many outweighs the needs of the few?''

'Thanks for the reminder, but you're forgetting one thing. I'm not the sole owner. My aunt has an interest in this venture, too.'

He raised one eyebrow. 'Aren't you willing to fight for what you know is right? Or do you always take the easy way out?'

She winced at the sting of his verbal barb. 'Selling the business is inevitable—'

'I don't care *who* owns the place,' he exploded. 'I object to you leaving the people without a local pharmacy in the meantime.'

'I'm not happy about it either,' she snapped. 'Spending Earl's nest egg on a losing proposition isn't a wise decision. I've discussed this at length with an extremely competent financial advisor who told me the same thing.' Tyler Fitzgerald had been a stockbroker before he taught economics and accounting at the high school.

'Ah,' Noah said knowingly, leaning against the counter. 'We've finally hit the crux of the matter. You're more worried about losing your money-in-the-hand inheritance than in investing it to help others.'

She rubbed the back of her neck as she closed her eyes.

Not true, she screamed inside. She didn't want a nickel of her uncle's—she didn't deserve it.

He raised an eyebrow. 'Going on a cruise, perhaps? Or maybe you're taking a Grand Tour of Europe?'

Her pride reared its head and she refused to argue her case any longer. He hadn't listened to her defense so far, much less attempted to understand her untenable position with her relative. In the struggle between honoring her uncle's wishes and appeasing her aunt, her aunt had won.

Eunice Ruscoe wanted her share of Earl's assets as soon as possible so she could shake the dust of Springwater off her feet for ever. Apparently she'd forgotten that the local dust hadn't touched her feet for the last fifteen years, not since she'd filed for a legal separation from her husband and moved to Topeka.

Jenny stared at him with defiance. 'That's a good idea. In fact, I may do both.'

A muscle twitched on the side of his face, and she took perverse pleasure in imagining the ache in his clenched jaw.

'I see I'm wasting my time.'

'I'm afraid so,' she said without apology.

He paused. 'I understand the obstacles you're facing, but Earl weathered his own share of storms. "Where there's a will, there's a way" was his motto. When the local economy was depressed from falling farm prices, he footed the tuition bill for several of Springwater's college kids. Over the years, at least twenty people benefited from his self-sacrifice.'

The number surprised her. Although her uncle had helped her with her own educational expenses, she hadn't realized he'd done the same for so many others.

'And at least three-fourths of them came back to live here after graduation. Earl Ruscoe saw a need and met it, sometimes at great personal sacrifice. Consider that when you dip into the little nest egg he left behind.'

He stormed away, his footsteps like thunderclaps in her ears before the bell tinkled behind him. Jenny sank bonelessly onto a vinyl-cushioned chair to stare at the prescription counter and listen to the echo of his departure.

*Where there's a will, there's a way.*

It didn't take much effort on her part to visualize her uncle's smiling face peering at her from underneath the PRESCRIPTION DROP-OFF sign. Hearing someone else repeat her uncle's infamous clichés seemed to drive home his absence.

*Do you always take the easy way out?*

Dr Kimball's accusation shook her out of her mental pity party. Maybe if she crunched the numbers, paid Herb's inflated salary out of her own savings... Maybe she could call a different professional head-hunter for a replacement... Surely there was a solution she'd overlooked, one that wouldn't require her returning to a profession she'd purposely left behind.

The same profession where mistakes proved costly in terms of human life.

No, she decided. She'd made her decision and people, especially Noah Kimball, would have to accept it.

The bell over the door jingled again. Certain Noah had returned to deliver another salvo, she squared her shoulders and turned to face him.

A familiar brunette entered with a dark-headed youngster at her side. Relieved that Noah hadn't returned, Jenny greeted her childhood friend warmly.

'Mary Beth? Is that you?'

The woman gave her a broad smile. 'I wasn't sure you'd remember me.'

'How could I forget? Uncle Earl always called us his Bobsey twins. His two-for-one summer special.'

Mary Beth giggled. 'I'd forgotten.' Her humor faded. 'I'm sorry we were out of town during the funeral. I would have been here if I'd known.'

'I understand.'

'And now you're closing.'

Jenny shrugged. 'I wish I didn't have to, but it can't be helped.' Not wanting to dwell on her loss or suffer through a plea to reconsider, she asked brightly, 'What can I do for you today?'

Mary Beth dug in her voluminous shoulder-strap hand-bag. 'I came to get Luke's prescription refilled.'

Although Jenny had known this moment would come—it was inevitable after Herb had resigned—she'd crossed her fingers that she wouldn't have to step into her old pharmacist role. She should have realized how ridiculous that hope was.

A feeling of panic rose in her throat, but she pasted a smile on her face. Her past mistakes didn't matter, she chided herself. Only the present did. Besides, this was a simple matter of counting out a few pills. She could do it. She *would* do it.

Jenny took the bottle Mary Beth handed her, praying that her friend wouldn't notice the slight tremor in her hand. 'Have a seat. It will only take a few minutes.'

Squaring her shoulders, she headed for the half-door separating the prescription department from the rest of the store. Her uncle's frayed and faded lab coat hung on a hook and she stared at it briefly, daunted by the prospect of what it meant if she slipped it on. Luke's high-pitched voice a few feet away reminded her that she had a job to do and no one else available to do it.

Resolutely, she donned the blue smock—blue because

he'd claimed the color wouldn't show the dirt as easily as white. Although a month had passed since he'd worn it, she could still smell his familiar Old Spice aftershave. Digging in one pocket, she found a handful of his favorite wintergreen Life-Savers.

In an instant, she remembered how she'd chided him for his cigarette habit. The very next day, he'd replaced his Marlboros with candy. All because she'd asked.

The memory brought tears to her eyes.

Shaking off her melancholy, she drew a bracing breath, then thumbed through the card files. Her uncle's system was archaic and a far cry from the computerized system of the hospital, but it worked.

Luke's original prescription for phenobarbital was still current, so she typed a new label and subtracted one of the two remaining refills. Next, she located the stock bottle on the shelf and counted out the correct number of tablets.

Once she'd finished she checked, double-checked, then finally triple-checked her work, before handing the small package to Mary Beth. If her friend thought it took longer than usual, she didn't comment.

'I see Luke has been on this for about six months,' Jenny commented.

Mary Beth nodded, ruffling her son's hair. 'Yes. He developed seizures at the time, although we still don't know why. As long as the phenobarbital controls them, we're happy.'

'Can we go, Mom?' Luke asked with a plaintive note to his voice. 'I'm gonna miss baseball practice.'

Jenny smiled at the eight-year-old boy as she rang up their purchase. 'Is he your only child?'

'Annie's three and Miranda's twelve. My husband manages the grocery store and I do the bookkeeping.' Mary

Beth counted out her money. 'I don't have to tell you how much we'll miss having your pharmacy in town. Remember when Earl served fountain drinks? Root beer floats were our specialty.'

Jenny thought of the solid walnut counter with its ornate hand-carved designs and bar stools that spun fast enough to compete with the rides at the county fair. She'd seen it just the other day under a protective tarp in her uncle's garage.

'Yeah,' she said fondly. 'It was a shame he did away with the snack business, but now I can understand why. Between the ice cream and soda pop that we either ate or spilled, I'm sure he lost more money than he made.'

'You were the one who pigged out on maraschino cherries,' Mary Beth accused with a smile. 'Those don't come cheap.'

Jenny laughed. 'Yeah, but we had a great time. We should have sold the recipes for some of our creations to Dairy Queen. We made Blizzards and Smoothies before they ever thought of them.'

Luke tugged on his mother's arm again. 'Mom. I'm *late*.'

'OK, OK,' she said. 'One more minute and I'll be done.'

He rolled his eyes, drooped his shoulders and shifted his weight as she asked Jenny another question. 'What will I need to do when Luke needs another refill?'

'I'm working on transferring the scripts to a pharmacy in Hays,' Jenny said apologetically, referring to the closest town. 'I know it won't be convenient…'

'We go quite often since my husband has family there, so I don't see a problem. You're the one I feel sorry for.'

'Me?' Jenny was incredulous. 'Why?'

Mary Beth gave her a sympathetic smile. 'After losing

your uncle, I can imagine how much fun you've had dealing with your aunt. Although I steered clear of her when we were kids, I doubt if her personality changed for the better after she moved away.'

Jenny grinned. 'It hasn't.'

'Well, hang in there and don't let her push you around. Even if you don't stay in town, please, keep in touch.'

'I'll try,' Jenny said.

Mary Beth and her son left just as another customer came in. As if word of the drug store closing had finally leaked out, a slow but steady stream of customers dropped in with requests for refills. Each one gave her an uneasy moment, but she dug in her mental heels and refused to let her old fears overtake her. She would take her time and do things right, she thought firmly. As she counted out an elderly man's lipid-lowering medication, she had a realization so startling that it made her hand freeze in mid-air.

She only had to answer to herself; no one would look over her shoulder and remind her to hurry along. In that instant, the black cloud hanging over her head seemed to disappear and her confidence—although still somewhat shaky—seemed to find a more solid footing.

Five o'clock arrived and Jenny gratefully flipped the OPEN sign to CLOSED. In spite of her reservations over filling in for Herb, she mentally patted herself on the back for a job well done. Her afternoon had been rather invigorating—her encounter with Noah notwithstanding—and she'd been pleasantly surprised that everything had run so smoothly. No one had complained about how slowly she'd worked either. Maybe she could make it through the next few days after all.

She reached to turn the deadbolt lock just as a young mother with a tow-headed toddler perched on her hip rushed to the glass door. As the woman caught sight of the CLOSED sign, her hopeful expression became downcast and her shoulders drooped with disappointment.

Jenny couldn't refuse her and sleep that night, so she let her inside.

'I know it's late, but can you fill this for me?' The woman, who couldn't have been more than twenty, spoke over her daughter's screams. Her shorts and shirt were threadbare but clean; her long blonde hair hung limp and lifeless. The youngster's clothes appeared equally worn, but a halo of tangled white-blonde curls surrounded her head.

'Yes, I can.' Jenny took the small prescription sheet from her latest customer. Instantly, she recognized the handwriting as Dr Kimball's, and deciphered the scrawl as an antibiotic.

'Daisy isn't feeling too well?' she asked, glancing at the child's flushed cheeks and tear-streaked face.

Her mother hoisted her higher on her hip. 'Another ear infection. She needs surgery to put those tubes in her ears, but we don't have the money right now. Randy—he's my husband—lost his job and we don't have insurance. We've applied for a medical card, but it takes a while to get one. After that, we'll get her fixed up.'

Jenny carefully reconstituted the powdered form of the antibiotic. It suddenly struck her how easily she'd stepped into her former role after a single afternoon. For a few seconds she toyed with the notion of taking over for Herb until she found a permanent replacement, but the idea didn't last. It might solve one problem, but it wouldn't alleviate the more pressing financial crunch her aunt had imposed.

Her job complete, she handed over the bottle. 'You can leave this at room temperature, Mrs Weir, but be sure to shake it well before you give her any. Also, Daisy gets one teaspoon twice a day for ten days. Don't stop, even if she feels better before then. Any questions?'

Mrs Weir shook her head. 'She's been on this before.'

'Good.' Jenny punched the numbers into the cash register. 'That will be twenty-seven ninety-five.'

The woman audibly inhaled and her face turned pale. 'Are you sure? It only cost me seven dollars last time I bought it.'

Jenny had covered for a retail pharmacist on occasion and had often heard customers complaining about high costs. Few antibiotics, however, sold for the price Mrs Weir had quoted. 'Newer medicines are rather expensive.'

As soon as her explanation left her mouth, Noah's comment echoed in her brain. *Your uncle was a generous man.* A suspicion suddenly took root as she considered the air of poverty clinging to the woman and child. 'If you'll wait a minute, I'll double-check.'

She disappeared behind the prescription counter and flipped through the account ledger until she found the page she wanted. As near as she could tell from past entries, he'd discounted nearly all of the meds for this family on a regular basis.

No wonder the pharmacy's finances were stretched to the point of breaking. If he subsidized everyone who experienced a cash-flow problem, it was nothing short of miraculous how he'd accumulated the fifteen thousand dollars in his saving account. Vowing to study his books in more detail, she returned to the checkout counter and found Mrs Weir crooning softly to her whimpering daughter.

'I'm sorry Daisy's so cranky, but when her ears hurt…'

Jenny smiled. 'I understand. As for the medicine, I mis-

read the price. There was a smudge on the label,' she
fibbed. 'Your bill today is seven dollars, even.'

'Oh, good.' Her relief took several worry lines off her
face. 'I just couldn't imagine the price going up that much
in a few weeks.'

Mrs Weir carefully counted out the five crumpled
greenbacks and a handful of change from her pocket, sigh-
ing in relief after she produced the right amount for her
purchase. Obviously, the woman had raided her cookie
jar, coat pockets, and the sofa cushions in order to gather
seven dollars.

As soon as Mrs Weir and Daisy left, Jenny sank onto
a chair to think. As much as she'd tried to follow Tyler's
directive to concern herself with the bottom line, she
couldn't. She'd entered the medical field because of a desire to help people. Even though she'd changed professions, she couldn't turn her back on the Mrs Weirs of the
world. Refusing a sick child his medicine because of a
parent's inability to pay rubbed against the grain of her
conscience.

Apparently, her uncle had suffered from the same moral
dilemma, which accounted for the reason his business had
fallen into dire straits.

At the same time, she wondered what Mrs Weir would
do if she had to fill her scripts in Hays, where no one
knew her or worried if she'd have enough money left over
to feed her family.

The prospect weighed heavily on her. Although she
didn't appreciate Noah Kimball's tactics, she grudgingly
admired him for fighting his patients' battles.

*Where there's a will, there's a way.*

Unfortunately, operating the pharmacy, even on a short-
term basis, required a courage she didn't possess. She

might have dispensed meds today without incident, but what about tomorrow? The next day, or the day after?

If she accepted the challenge Noah had thrown before her, how would she appease her aunt? How could she meet her commitment to Susan?

'Focus on what you *can* do,' she scolded herself aloud as she shut off all the lights, except for the one over her uncle's scarred oak desk. She sat down and reached for her day planner, flipping to the telephone directory. With a little bit of luck and a lot of inspiration, she'd figure out what that would be before she left for Grand Junction on Saturday.

On Monday afternoon, Noah returned from his luncheon Rotary Club meeting with his previously good spirits somewhat dampened. He'd hoped for the speculation surrounding the Ruscoe Pharmacy to die a natural death after Jennifer had packed up and left town on Saturday, but it hadn't. The men had talked of nothing else until their president had finally called the group to order.

While the news of Earl's financial hard times had been surprising to everyone, Noah didn't believe the situation had progressed to an unsalvageable stage. In time and with proper management, Earl's legacy could once again have become profitable.

Unfortunately, time had run out, which meant that he had to step in. He was used to picking up the pieces that others—his father, his former fiancée—had left behind.

Toward the end of last week, he'd called every pharmaceutical rep he knew—and some he didn't—hoping to entice them into considering a business opportunity in Springwater. While none had seemed interested in the venture for themselves, they'd promised to spread the word.

Satisfied by his efforts to set prospective change in motion, something about Jennifer's career switch still nagged at him. Earl had related countless stories of how Jennifer had overcome difficulties to achieve her goals. She'd worked hard and earned a basketball scholarship. She'd struggled with her chemistry classes, but hadn't given up because she'd needed those for her pharmacy degree. It seemed odd for her to have given up the profession she'd supposedly held dear.

However, given that as her history, he could understand why her pride had prevented her from sharing the details of her failure with her uncle. He didn't condone her decision, but at least he understood her motives.

However, he wasn't as quick to forgive her blatant refusal to follow through on her own promise to her dying relative. It reminded him of too many other empty pledges he'd heard in his lifetime.

His father would promise anything to avoid conflict at any given moment. Once Noah had learned this—and it hadn't taken too many years—he'd sworn to be different when he grew up. As he'd matured into adolescence, he'd worked hard to become a man of his word, spurred on by the fear of living up to his father's reputation and being labelled as the proverbial chip off the old block.

As an adult, the experience of being left at the altar to deal with three hundred wedding guests and half as many gifts had sealed his hatred of broken promises.

The big question in his mind now was why she hadn't applied her tenacity to Earl's business. Why had she given up so easily?

The obvious answer was that she didn't care. However, he'd never know her real reasons because she'd packed her bags and left town without any forwarding address.

With luck, it wouldn't be long before someone else recognized the potential gold mine and capitalized on it.

In the meantime, he wanted to put the entire incident—including his inopportune flashbacks of holding Jennifer in his arms whenever he saw a tall, copper-haired woman with shapely legs—behind him and concentrate on the future.

He strode into his clinic via the private staff entrance in the rear of the building and found his three employees—Della Sutton, his office manager, Tanya Carmichael, the receptionist, and Karen Carson, his nurse—huddled together in Tanya's cubicle.

'Having a powwow?' he asked as he stood in the doorway, curious about their intense discussion.

Della looked up at him, her brown eyes shining with undisguised excitement. A petite dishwater-blonde in her mid-fifties, she'd been a godsend ever since he'd moved to Springwater nearly two years ago.

'It's about time you got back from lunch,' she declared.

'My meeting ran long,' he said. 'I used to think women cornered the market on gossip, but after today I've changed my mind. What's wrong?'

She waved her hand, as if dismissing his question. 'We're dying to know what's happening over at Ruscoe's Pharmacy.'

He groaned. 'Oh, please. Not you, too.'

Karen, twenty-five and wearing a sparkling gold wedding band, joined in. 'Of course everyone wants to talk about the drug store. It's big news.'

He frowned. 'I haven't heard anything today that I would consider as "big" news. Is someone else taking over?' It would be great if his efforts to attract another owner had paid off so quickly.

'Not that we know of. We think Jenny's not going out of business after all,' Karen reported importantly.

He shook his head. 'Wishful thinking, ladies. Anyone who pins his hopes on Jennifer is setting himself up for disappointment. Besides, what makes you think she's changed her mind?'

Tanya, a nineteen-year-old blonde who'd started working for him right after she'd graduated from high school the previous year, stared up at him from her chair behind the reception desk. Her wide eyes gleamed with excitement.

'The "Going Out of Business" sign is down. In fact, it was gone on Saturday morning.'

'So it fell down,' he said, being practical.

'I thought so, too, at first,' Tanya said. 'Then I noticed something odd. If her sign had fallen, it would have been on the floor by the window. The poster wasn't there. Totally disappeared. Like someone had carried it away.' She shivered. 'It reminds me of the book I just finished, *Midnight is for Murder*. The detective discovered the witness had—'

'Let's not get melodramatic,' he interrupted. Tanya's passion for mystery novels turned every unusual event into a plot to be solved. 'You can't believe that life will revert back to normal because a sign is missing. I'm sure there's a simple, logical explanation.'

Karen broke in. 'It's not just the sign. My dad was the officer on patrol Wednesday night. He was worried over the light being on so late when it normally isn't. With the place having drugs and all, the officers always keep close tabs on that particular block. Anyway, Jenny stayed at the store until two in the morning.'

'Ladies, ladies,' he said in a long-suffering tone. 'You're reading more into this than you should. I'm sure

Jennifer had a lot to do. Pharmaceuticals to return, paperwork to complete, that sort of thing.'

Della stood with her hands planted on her hips. 'Then how do you explain her trips to the bank both on Thursday and Friday? The trips where she spent several hours with Tom Rigby, the loan officer?'

Noah grinned at how reverently Della spoke Tom's name. 'Didn't he spill all the details during your date Friday night?' After being widowed three years ago, Della had started seeing Tom on a regular basis.

Della stuck her nose in the air. 'I'll have you know, Tom won't betray a confidence. All he said was that they were discussing business.'

'Well, then—' Noah began.

The door burst open and Harriet Winkler crossed the threshold. Although the sixty-eight-year-old lady walked with a cane, her steps were brisk. She wore a casual cotton dress and her trade-mark straw hat had purple silk flowers attached to the headband.

'You'll never guess what I just saw,' she announced.

'What?' Noah's three employees echoed.

Harriet preened with her information, the flowers on her head quivering from excitement. A retired teacher and current owner of Gently Read Books, she knew more about the locals than anyone else in town.

She ambled to the receptionist's window and leaned through the opening. 'A moving van pulled up in front of Earl's house two hours ago. His niece is carrying boxes *inside*. What do you make of that?'

Noah rolled his eyes, wondering if everyone had lost their grip on reality. Either that, or he'd stepped into an episode of *The Twilight Zone*. 'A person can't pack without boxes. They have to get inside somehow.'

Harriet pursed her mouth, making her wrinkled face

resemble a prune. 'I've seen enough people moving in my day to know one thing. If a person needs a dolly to move an empty box, then I'll eat my hat. Nope.' She shook her head for emphasis. 'Little Jenny Ruscoe is moving in. From the things I saw her unload, she's staying for some time.'

# CHAPTER THREE

TANYA faced Noah. 'See there? Everything adds up. Just like we said.'

He let out a disgusted sigh. 'Oh, for the love of—'

Della held up her hands. 'Now, now, Dr Doubting Thomas. I think you should check things out for yourself.'

'I did,' he said crossly, still smarting from his failed attempt to talk sense into her. 'If Jennifer Ruscoe is moving into Earl's house, it's strictly on a temporary basis. She isn't interested in Springwater or its residents. Now, can we, *please*, get to work?'

Tanya and Karen fell silent. Their faces collectively turned pink at his scolding, their hopeful and happy moods crushed by his harsh comment.

Even Harriet's smile faltered while Tanya clamped her lips into a hard line and began entering Harriet's name into the computer. Karen slipped out of the cubicle like a wraith and he pushed away his remorse for destroying their fantasy. Facts, however unpleasant, had to be accepted.

Della, however, was the only one who didn't act intimidated by his harsh words. She rose from her perch on Tanya's desk and glared at him. 'It's entirely possible for Jenny to change her mind, you know.'

'Yeah,' he admitted, watching Karen usher Harriet into the treatment room across the hall. 'But she doesn't want to sink any of her inheritance into her family's business, so I doubt if she has.'

Considering the subject closed, he met Karen outside

the door. 'She's ready for you,' the nurse said, before she disappeared around the corner. Her averted gaze and whipped-puppy manner made him feel like an ogre.

He stepped inside, reading the notes Karen had recorded. 'You're getting around much better than the last time I saw you, Harriet.'

Harriet stuck out her right leg. Her knee, which had been red, swollen and tender to touch, now appeared symptom-free. 'Oh, I am. I can get around so much better now. I'm able to work in my store, too, instead of lying in bed with an ice pack. Which reminds me, Gina saved you a copy of Tom Clancy's latest, so you can pick it up any time.'

'I'll drop by in the next day or two.' He reviewed the page of her most recent lab results. 'The synovial fluid I removed from your knee the other day was positive for uric acid crystals, which translates into what we call gout. This wasn't your first episode, if I remember right.'

'No. I've had this off and on for the last five years. Although my last attack hit me shortly before I became your patient.'

'According to your blood work, your uric acid level is too high. To bring it down, I'm going to prescribe a drug called allopurinol, which should slow your body's production of uric acid. Are you having any side effects to the colchicine you started taking last week?'

'Some,' she said. 'A little nausea and diarrhea.'

'I'll lower your dosage until we stabilize the blood levels with the allopurinol. After a few months, if you don't have any attacks and the uric acid stays in the normal range, we'll discontinue the colchicine. Also, keep taking a non-steroidal anti-inflammatory drug, like ibuprofen or naproxen. Drink plenty of fluids, too.'

'OK.'

'Any other problems?'

Harriet shook her head. 'No, but I started going for regular massages to work the kinks out of this old body. I don't need to stop, do I?'

'Not at all.'

'Good,' she said. 'There's nothing more relaxing than a good massage. Have you had one?'

He flipped the chart closed. 'No, I haven't.'

'Then, by all means, you should try it. You don't know what you're missing.'

He grinned at her solemn expression. 'I'll keep it in mind.'

'I'm serious,' she insisted. 'I imagine it's stressful to have people asking you about Earl's business all the time. Why, I could tell a few minutes ago how frustrated you are over the whole situation. I understand why you don't want to hear any more talk on the subject.'

Something in her tone warned him. 'But you're going to comment anyway,' he guessed.

She smiled. 'I always knew you were a smart man. Actually, I want to plant a few things for you to think about. You see, being a teacher for thirty-some years, I've learned to read people. You've heard the cliché about how the eyes are the window to the soul.'

'Yes. So?'

'Have you ever looked in Jenny's eyes, Noah?'

As a matter of fact, he had stared into them on several occasions. Over the past month, he'd seen a lot of emotion in those blue-gray depths—emotion ranging from the anguish he'd seen at Earl's passing to a fiery anger that matched the vibrant hues of her hair.

He didn't like his attraction to Jennifer's outer package. 'What's your point?'

'Jenny may come across as being tough and unsympathetic, but she isn't. I think she cares too much about people and their situations and so she purposely distances herself.'

He inwardly disagreed. He'd tried to appeal to her compassion and it hadn't made any impression. Either she was as hard-hearted as he'd imagined, or she'd buried her compassionate side far deeper than he cared to dig. He suspected it was the former.

'It's also been said that actions speak louder than words,' he reminded her.

'Sometimes a person has to do something she doesn't want to do.'

He stared at her in disbelief. 'If you're trying to convince me that Jennifer doesn't want to abandon the business, you're going to fail.'

'What did she say when you talked to her last week?'

'Let's see.' He counted off on his fingers. 'The building needs repairs, her inventory isn't up to standard, she lost her help. I know those things take money, but she refuses to invest Earl's own nest egg to keep his dream alive.'

Harriet paused, clearly considering his comment. 'I know a lot of people are placing blame on Jenny,' she began, 'but how well do you know Eunice Ruscoe?'

'Not at all,' he admitted, thinking back to the first time he'd seen the woman which had been at Earl's funeral. Tall, like Earl, she bore a remarkable resemblance both in appearance and personality to a crow. She'd worn a perpetual frown on her face and had found fault with everything from the flowers to the church service itself.

'She's always begrudged every minute and every dime that Earl spent on his business. It was the one thing in his life that he controlled totally and it bothered her like a festering sore. Now, after inheriting half of his estate, she finally has her chance to make up for all those years.

Believe me, as hateful as she is, she isn't about to turn loose any funds for improvements.'

Although her explanation seemed plausible, he wasn't ready to let Jennifer off the hook so easily. 'You're guessing.'

She shrugged. 'Maybe. But I've known her for years. I know what she's like.'

'If you're right about the two of them, then how do you explain Jennifer's change of heart?'

'To those of us who have faith in Jenny, her reasons don't matter. But if you need a reason, turn on your charm to find it. Show her you aren't her enemy. Eventually, she'll tell you whatever you want to know.'

Jennifer was a beautiful woman and under other circumstances he wouldn't have found 'turning on the charm' a hardship at all. Now, however, the idea seemed hypocritical when her personality embodied everything he despised—greed, selfishness, and lack of compassion. Obviously Harriet colored her view of Jennifer from her childhood and not recent events.

'Before you throw me out of the room for meddling,' she said with a faint smile, 'can you do me a favor? Please, keep an open mind. If Jenny has found a way to appease her aunt—and you—then give her a chance.'

'I suppose you won't be happy unless I agree.'

Harriet smiled. 'No.'

He hesitated as he weighed her suggestion. 'I'll try.' It was the most he could promise.

'That's all anyone can ask.' She tried to push herself out of the chair and Noah came to her rescue. 'Since we've settled that, when do I need to come back and hear you tell me how well I'm doing?'

Noah laughed at her impertinence. Harriet was the only person in town—other than Della—who could get away with lecturing him. 'Two weeks. We'll do another blood test to check your uric acid and adjust the dosage of your medication accordingly.'

'I'll be here,' she declared, placing the hat on her head as Noah walked beside her. She stopped at the door. 'You won't forget what I told you?'

As if he could. 'No.'

'Good.' She sounded satisfied. 'Jenny really is a pretty young woman.'

He couldn't disagree, even though he wanted to. In fact, he'd made the same observation the first time Earl had shown off her picture like a proud parent.

'Your age, too, if I'm not mistaken.'

'She's still a baby.' He didn't consider a six years' age difference as being significant, but he wanted to discourage Harriet's matchmaking attempts.

Harriet's eyes twinkled. 'She's the most mature infant I've ever seen.'

He nearly groaned aloud as he remembered her soft curves pressed against his chest. Her smooth skin had seemed like silk and the scent of berries clinging to her hair had given him a respite from the harsh odor of disinfectant and death.

'And speaking of babies, Jenny's going to have beautiful ones someday. Mark my words, they'll look just like her. In fact, you might get to deliver them.' She reached out and patted his arm. 'Now, don't forget to pick up your book.'

'I won't.' He watched her leave, shaking his head at her obvious attempt to pique his interest in Jennifer. It would take a lot more to change his mind than an old neighbor vouching for her and talking of beautiful copper-haired, blue-eyed babies. Everyone else might believe her excuses, but he wouldn't. He'd been fed a steady diet of those during various times of his life and he refused to swallow them so easily.

Karen passed him in the corridor. 'When you're through wool-gathering, I have several patients waiting.'

Her cool tone suggested that she still hadn't forgiven him for the episode in Tanya's office. He'd have to eat a slice of humble pie if he wanted to crawl back into his staff's good graces.

A break in his routine came when seven-year-old Blair Bright walked in beside his mother, sobbing as he clutched his right forearm. 'What do we have here?' he asked the skinny child whose large plastic-rimmed glasses lent him a scholarly rather than a sportsman-like air.

Mrs Bright wrung her hands. 'I feel terrible. Blair is shy and I finally talked him into rollerblading with the boy next door. Ten minutes later, he falls and hurts his arm. I think it's broken.'

'Could be,' Noah said. 'Those things happen, but let's take a look.'

Blair sniffled as Noah examined his forearm and wrist. 'I was wearing all my pads, and I still got hurt,' he said, sounding aggrieved by the apparent failure of his safety equipment.

'That was a smart thing to do,' Noah told him. 'Just think how much worse you could feel if you hadn't worn your gear.'

Blair's mouth formed an 'O' as he pondered this new slant to the situation. 'You're right,' he said, his tears instantly drying. 'I could have skinned my knees and my elbows, too, but I didn't.'

Noah smiled as he ruffled the boy's light brown hair. 'I'm going to take a few X-rays and then we'll decide what to do. OK?'

Blair nodded. In no time at all, Noah had pictures to

prove that all bones were intact. Diagnosing a bad sprain, he immobilized the boy's arm and sent the tired youngster home with his less anxious mother.

Shortly before five o'clock, Karen ushered in his last patient of the day. 'I see my favorite person has come to visit me,' he told Daisy Weir. The little girl giggled before she buried her face in her mother's chest.

Violet smiled. 'As you can see, she's much better.'

Noah scooted the small stool close to the exam table. 'May I peek in your ears, Daisy?'

The youngster stuck her thumb in her mouth and nodded. Without hesitation, she turned her head while Noah quickly checked her ear canal with his otoscope.

'Looks almost normal,' he said. 'But we really need to organize a long-term solution for her. Living on antibiotics isn't good for her immune system.'

'Randy got a job this weekend, working on a harvest crew,' Violet said. 'We can probably afford her surgery soon.'

'Then I'll make an appointment with Dr Colyer, the ENT specialist. In the meantime, make sure she finishes the antibiotic we started last week.'

'I will,' she promised. 'You know, I was really impressed by the lady pharmacist we have. She was so nice to us.'

*Nice?* He paused in his note-taking to listen while Violet continued.

'We didn't get there until she was closing, but she let us in anyway and filled Daisy's prescription.'

'Sounds like you were lucky to catch her.'

'Oh, we were. What was even nicer was how she treated us after I caught her overcharging me.'

His mental antennae quivered. He wondered how many other people had paid too much for their medications because they hadn't questioned the fee. 'She overcharged you?'

'Uh-huh. After I said that twenty-seven dollars couldn't be right because I only paid seven for the same prescription before, she looked it up in her book and corrected it without a fuss. Said she misread the bottle.'

Noah's outrage turned to puzzlement. The antibiotic he'd prescribed was one of the third generation of penicillins, which made it fairly expensive. The price Jennifer had quoted sounded about right. By accepting the lower payment, she had literally given away the medication.

The gesture seemed out of character, yet it confirmed Harriet's opinion of her soft heart. If she was right about that, was it possible for Harriet to be right about other things, too? That Jenny was moving *into* and not *out of* Earl's house? If so, then Jennifer might be keeping her promise to her uncle after all.

He shouldn't care what had happened behind the scenes in the past week as long as she stayed in business, but he did. His need to protect Earl's interests and those of his patients overshadowed his desire to discover the real Jennifer Ruscoe. Or so he told himself.

Deciding on the spur of the moment to track her down that very day, he sent the Weirs home, shucked his white coat and left on his mission.

Jenny juggled two ungainly boxes and her shoulder-bag in order to unlock the back door of the drug store. 'Come on in, Carrie,' she told the bright-eyed, dark-haired eleven-year-old as she dropped her bulky load to flick on the light switches. 'I want to show you around.'

Carrie stepped over the threshold, craning her neck to dubiously ogle her surroundings. 'I didn't realize this

place was so *old*. I thought it would be more like the
pharmacy we go to at home.'

Thinking of the store recently built a few blocks from
the apartment complex where she and the Fentons lived,
Jenny knew her uncle's—no, *her*—operation was as different from the national chain's as night and day.

'After we finish our fix-it projects, the place will look
a lot better. Go on. Make yourself at home.'

Carrie didn't need another invitation. She immediately
poked her nose into every drawer and shelf, like a man
hunting for buried treasure. It must have been ages since
Earl had sifted through his stock, so Carrie would easily
occupy her time and attention for the next few weeks.

Given her love of organizing things, bringing Carrie
here for the summer was perfect for all concerned. After
they finished with the main floor, the entire basement
begged for the same treatment. It, however, wasn't a priority, but Jenny knew Carrie would be delighted to tackle
the job. Creepy-crawlies didn't bother her a bit—a trait
which would come in handy as they worked downstairs.

Jenny turned down the thermostat, pleased to hear the
air-conditioning kick into action. No matter what happened between now and September, at least she'd work
in comfort.

Provided she could pay the electricity bill.

Pushing aside the concern, she followed Carrie as the
youngster walked through the area where they stored their
prescription drugs and into the main store. 'As you can
see, we have our work cut out for us.'

Carrie picked up a dust-laden teddy bear and wrinkled
her nose just before she sneezed. 'I'll say! How old is this
stuff?'

Jenny smiled. 'Older than you are, I'm sure. That's why
we're going to give everything a face-lift. No one will

recognize us as being the same store by the time we're done.' Surely a buyer would look more favorably on them if he saw a more modernized facility.

Carrie sat the bear next to its companion and eyed her surroundings. 'You've already told me what you want to do, but I'm only here for six weeks. It's gonna take longer than that.'

'It looks like a big project right now,' Jenny admitted, 'but once we get started it won't be so bad. With two pairs of hands, we'll accomplish twice as much in half the time.' She refused to let negative thoughts infect her high hopes, especially since she had so much riding on the outcome.

Once again, Carrie didn't appear convinced. 'If you say so.' She glanced around. 'Are you wanting to start on this tonight?'

Jenny heard the dread in Carrie's voice. They'd worked hard to unload and unpack their things at her uncle's—her—house and they were both tired.

'Just look around for now,' she said. 'We'll start fresh in the morning. I'll make a new sign for the window and then we'll grab something to eat before we call it a day.'

Carrie might enjoy a relaxing evening, but Jenny still had one important appointment to keep—a meeting that required her personal attention—before she could slide between the sheets.

While Carrie wandered around, Jenny found the end roll of newsprint she'd bought and a package of magic markers. She tore off a large section, placed it on the floor, and sat Indian-style in front of it.

The words for her new sign came easier and with a lot less emotional torment.

'New hours. Monday through Friday. 11 to 5 p.m.'

Under ideal circumstances, she would have remained

closed until she'd completed the most involved remodeling projects, but people would still need their prescriptions filled, whether she was open for business or not. This way, she could keep Noah Kimball happy and not lose any income, however small it might be.

As for Dr Kimball, now that time had let her view the situation more objectively, she grudgingly admired him for his protective interest in the pharmacy's fate. In spite of their discord, she couldn't find fault with a doctor whose actions were motivated out of genuine concern for his patients, even if he was opinionated and over-bearing.

'Jenny?' Carrie called out from across the room as Jenny carefully printed her message. 'There's a lady outside, wanting in. She looks mad, too.'

Filled with a sense of impending doom, Jenny scrambled to her feet. Her aunt's cupped hands framed her sour face as she peered through the plate-glass window.

Jenny inwardly groaned. Eunice was early, *much* too early, and Jenny hadn't mentally prepared herself for their meeting. How like Eunice to ignore their arrangements and then act inconvenienced because Jenny wasn't at the appointed place.

She quickly unlocked the front door and forced a cheerful note in her voice. 'Aunt Eunice. What a surprise. Is it seven o'clock already?'

'No, it's not,' Eunice snapped, her black pillbox hat perched on top of gray hair worn in her usual tight bun. Jenny had made the mistake one summer of allowing her aunt to put her hair up, and had paid the price. Her headache had lasted for a week and her eyelids had taken just as long to feel normal and not slanted.

Eunice's black suit was reminiscent of the sixties, probably because she'd owned it since then. She purchased fabrics guaranteed for long wear and totally ignored current fashion. Since she kept all of her clothes for years, the styles eventually came back into vogue. To Jenny's knowledge, the last time Eunice had bought a new dress had been in 1975 for Twyla Beach's daughter's wedding. Since then, she'd never passed up an opportunity to complain about the cost.

'I wanted to get home before dark,' Eunice stated, 'so I came early. Although any time I'd hoped to gain I lost looking for you. Why I let you talk me into coming by this late at night, I'll never know.'

The idea of talking Eunice into doing anything that she didn't want to do was ludicrous. Nothing ruled her aunt except her own wishes. As for it being late, the large wall clock showed five-fifteen.

'I offered to save you a trip and mail the check,' Jenny reminded her, who'd been willing to fork out the extra fees required for certified and registered mail. The money spent would have been worth the opportunity to avoid dealing with her aunt in person.

Eunice snorted. 'As if I'd trust the US postal service with my inheritance.' Her eyes narrowed. 'You *do* have it with you, don't you?'

'Yes.' Jenny motioned to Carrie whose instincts had apparently warned her to keep her distance. The youngster approached with a wary look in her eyes.

'Would you, please, get my bag?' Jenny asked her. 'It's on the desk.'

Carrie nodded as she scampered to obey.

'Who's she?' Eunice demanded to know.

'My friend's daughter. She's spending a few weeks with me while her mother finishes her research project and thesis.'

Eunice's mouth fell into a disapproving line. 'I might

have known. Another woman who can't take care of her own brats and pawns them off on someone else.'

Jenny stiffened, aware of Eunice's backhanded slur against Jenny's mother. She'd loved spending her summers with her uncle since he'd been her only link to her father's family. She'd enjoyed them even more after her aunt had moved out of town.

'You're wrong,' Jen said coldly. 'Susan is a friend in need.'

Eunice sniffed. 'That's what Earl would say before he took in every stray he could possibly find. Both of you are just too soft-hearted for your own good. It must be in your blood.'

'Why, thank you,' Jenny said, knowing her aunt hadn't meant to be complimentary. She wanted to add that being soft-hearted was much better than being mean-spirited and growing old alone, but in the interests of peace she kept silent. After she transferred these funds, Jenny didn't plan on seeing her aunt for any reason ever again.

Carrie rushed forward with the bag in both hands and passed it over. 'Thanks, hon,' Jenny said, tugging on Carrie's ponytail.

'You're welcome.'

Carrie skipped back to whatever had occupied her interest before being interrupted while Jenny withdrew two white envelopes from her bag. Handing one to her aunt, she said, 'It's a cashier's check. Just like you wanted.'

Eunice's eyes brightened as she eagerly snatched it out of Jenny's grip. Apparently greed was the only emotion she could experience with any degree of enthusiasm. She tore open the flap and studied the figures. In the next instant, she reverted back to her contemptuous self. 'Such a paltry sum for a lifetime of work,' she said.

'It's exactly one-half of Earl's estate.' Jenny had the

appraisal to prove it. She removed the page from the en-
velope in her hand and snatched an ink pen off the
counter, wishing all of this had been handled under Terrell
Hawver's legal eye. He'd prepared the actual sale papers
and personally obtained the necessary signatures. The
forms awaiting Eunice's signature today were a mere for-
mality to show that she had received her share of the
money.

'If you'll sign here on the dotted line, everything will
be finalized.'

Eunice refused the pen to glance around the room. 'I
see you're going ahead with your foolhardy idea of running this place.'

'Yes.' Jenny dangled the pen under Eunice's nose. Take
it and sign, she mentally urged, feeling a sheen of nervous
perspiration form across her forehead at the delay.

'Maybe I shouldn't let you buy me out after all.'

Jenny crossed the fingers on her free hand. If Eunice
knew how much Jenny wanted to cut all ties—especially
the financial ones—she'd refuse to sell her portion even
at this late date. Terrell might have the notarized bill of
sale in his safe, but Eunice was crafty enough to spot any
loopholes Terrell might have missed.

'That's your choice,' she said evenly, hoping Eunice
wouldn't see through her act of indifference. 'I can certainly put your portion of the money to good use. I'm
short on inventory and the remodeling alone will take a
huge chunk of change. Rewiring is so expensive, but it
has to be done. We can't risk an electrical fire. Being a
businesswoman yourself, you're aware of how one must
spend money in order to make it.'

Jenny reached out and lightly pinched the edge of Eunice's check between her thumb and forefinger.

Eunice snatched the cashier's check away and tucked

it into her black patent leather handbag for safekeeping. 'Where do I sign?'

Jenny bit back a relieved sigh as she once again held out the pen and pointed to the appropriate line on the form. 'Right here.' Without realizing it, she held her breath until Eunice had scrawled her name on the document.

'Don't think you can come crawling to me for a hand-out when you can't make a go of it,' Eunice warned on her way to the front entrance. 'I'm not a bank.'

It had been a well-known secret that as an only child of an only child, she'd inherited a vast sum from her own relatives. She could easily afford to give up her parsi-monious ways for the rest of her life and still live in style, even if she lived to be a hundred and twenty.

'Don't worry, I won't.' Jenny opened the door. 'Have a safe trip.'

Eunice stuck her nose in the air and marched out. Jenny didn't waste any time sliding the deadbolt home.

Carrie joined her and the two of them watched Eunice drive away in her white Mercedes. 'I'm awful glad she left. I was afraid she'd be here for *hours*.'

Jenny shuddered at the thought. 'Me, too, squirt. Thank heavens she wasn't.'

'She's not a nice lady.'

'No, she's not.'

'Was she always this grouchy?'

'For as long as I can remember,' Jenny said honestly.

Carrie's eyes widened. 'Gosh. I can't imagine *wanting* to live with someone like her.'

A deep sadness filled Jenny as she contemplated how Eunice had made her beloved uncle's life a living hell. He'd deserved someone far better than the woman he'd married. As for herself, she'd learned a valuable lesson—

it was better to never marry than to marry the wrong person.

'Neither can I,' Jenny admitted.

'Maybe something happened a long time ago and it made her grumpy.'

Jenny smiled down on Carrie. 'Could be, but I've never heard. Some people just aren't happy unless they're making other people's lives miserable. I'm afraid my aunt is one of them.'

'Too bad. She's missing out on a lot.'

For a kid, Carrie had remarkable insight. 'You're right, she is.' Pushing aside the maudlin thoughts, Jenny clapped her hands together. 'Give me a few more minutes to hang my sign, and then we'll go.'

She'd crouched down to pick the poster off the floor and noticed a shadow falling over her shoulder. She glanced up and nearly lost her balance at the sight of her latest—and equally unwelcome—visitor.

Jenny rose, finger-combing her hair away from her face. 'How did you get in?' she demanded. After dealing with her aunt, she wasn't in the mood to match wits with Noah Kimball. And since she had an impressionable audience, she didn't want to stage a repeat performance of their earlier shouting match.

He shrugged. 'Through the door.'

'It's locked.'

'The back door isn't.'

'It's not for customers. Private use only.'

'I'm not a customer,' he pointed out.

His face revealed something she couldn't quite define— uncertainty, sympathy… A horrible idea took hold.

She glanced in Carrie's direction, hoping a trinket had captured her interest, but it hadn't. She stood in the far corner and studied the two of them with undisguised curiosity.

Jenny lowered her voice and narrowed her eyes as she pinned her most frosty gaze on him. 'How long have you been listening?'

He hesitated for only a few seconds. 'Long enough.'

# CHAPTER FOUR

NOAH watched a variety of emotions flit across Jennifer's face—horror, embarrassment, then outrage—before she raised her chin to a stubborn angle.

'Is eavesdropping a habit of yours?'

'No, but when I walked in, you and your aunt were deep in your...' he cleared his throat '...your discussion. I didn't feel I should interrupt.' He'd told himself to leave and wait for her outside near her car, but he'd been so stunned by the specifics of their conversation that his feet had somehow become rooted to the floor.

'I suppose I can expect the whole town to know what went on by morning,' she said bitterly.

'I hear rumors, but I *don't* spread them.'

She didn't appear convinced, although he understood why she didn't trust him. He'd either avoided her for the past month or vented his anger on her. After overhearing Eunice's comments, he was more confused about Jennifer Ruscoe than ever.

Then again, maybe he wasn't ready to admit that he'd misjudged her—that she really *did* care about Earl's legacy and the needs of the community.

She motioned in Carrie's direction. 'If you're here to create a scene, forget it. I won't let you upset her.'

He held up his hands in surrender. 'That's not my intent. I stopped by because people have been speculating about you all day. I want to separate fact from fiction.'

'I'm sure the facts aren't nearly as interesting as the stories.'

'Maybe not, but the truth has a way of easing people's worries.'

'All right. All right. I can see you won't rest until you've asked whatever is on your mind, so go ahead,' she said crossly as she folded her arms against her chest and tapped one foot impatiently against the tile.

'Let's see.' He ticked off the points on his fingers. 'First of all, they say you're not closing.' He pointed to her sign on the floor. 'It looks like one rumor's true.'

Surprise flashed across her face. 'I can't imagine how that could be making the rounds already. Unless Tom at the bank said something to someone.'

Noah thought of Della. 'He hasn't mentioned a word.'

She frowned, as if contemplating how the story might have leaked out. 'Then how—?'

'Your original "Going Out of Business" notice disappeared.'

'That's quite an assumption to make from such flimsy evidence.'

'My receptionist considers herself an amateur detective,' he added wryly. 'Between the missing poster, your late hours and people seeing you in the bank on several occasions last week, they drew their own conclusions.'

'If everyone keeps such close tabs on everything they see and hear, Springwater doesn't need a newspaper.'

He grinned. 'We don't have one. Most people subscribe to the *Hays Daily*. Their staff does a good job of covering our local events and anything else that comes along.'

'Like an old business under new management?'

'Exactly. I can make a phone call and you'll be featured in Sunday's business section.'

'Thanks, but this place isn't ready for publicity yet,' she said, glancing around the store. 'Maybe in a few weeks.'

'How long are you keeping those hours?' he asked, motioning to her poster.

'It all depends on how quickly the contractors finish the remodeling and repairs. Have I answered all of your questions?' she asked, her tone clearly one of dismissal.

'No.'

She stared at him. 'There's more?'

Noah nodded. 'I understand you're here to stay.'

She raised an eyebrow. 'I can't commute from Grand Junction, you know.'

'To stay long term,' he corrected.

'Your source is wrong,' she said flatly, as her gaze drifted across the room. 'I've moved in, but I'm strictly a temporary resident. I'll be leaving in the fall, after I turn the store over to someone else.'

'What made you change your mind? I thought you didn't want to be bothered by all of this.' He gestured as he glanced around the room.

'Thinking about taking credit for influencing me?'

His denial was vehement.

'Why does it matter what changed my mind? If memory serves me...' she tapped her temple '...you didn't care who provided the pharmacy services, only that those services were provided. I simply chose to temporarily fill in the gap.'

'I'm curious. That's all. You made it sound like you were on the verge of bankruptcy, yet you've obviously bought out your aunt's portion.'

She paused to nibble on her lower lip. For a few moments he thought she might break down and confide in him, but her expression changed. She'd obviously talked herself out of using him as a sounding-board.

When she spoke again her voice was laced with quiet strength. 'Uncle Earl taught me a valuable lesson about dealing with the public. Never discuss religion, politics, or finances. I won't deny that money will be tight for a while, but the status of my bank account is none of your business, Dr Kimball.'

'If you're strapped for cash, I know of someone who'd be willing to underwrite your venture.'

She raised one eyebrow. 'Who? You?'

His offer had been impulsive and he was surprised she'd guessed correctly. 'Why not? I can always use an investment.'

'Isn't that a conflict of interest?'

He thought quickly. 'Not if I invest in the building. It's not my fault that a pharmacy just happens to occupy the space.'

Carrie walked toward them, carefully holding a small music box. 'Hey, Jenny. Look at this. Isn't this neat?'

Jenny took the little ballerina with the faded red net skirt and dutifully admired it from every angle. 'Very pretty.'

'And she works, too.' Carrie wound the key several turns. The dancer slowly pivoted to a tinny rendition of the 'Blue Danube' waltz. 'What are we going to do with all of this neat stuff?'

'Most of this ''neat stuff'' isn't worth keeping, much less selling,' Jenny said. 'We'll probably throw most of it away.'

Carrie's face registered her horror. 'Oh, we can't do that. Why don't we have a garage sale?'

Jenny didn't appear enthusiastic. 'You get very little in return for all the work it takes to get ready.'

Noah couldn't keep silent. 'One man's junk is another man's treasure.'

'Yeah, right,' Carrie seconded, flashing him a big smile

which he returned. 'I'd bet we'd earn more money than you think, too.'

Jenny shook her head as she glared at him. She obviously didn't appreciate the way he'd sided with her young charge. 'We don't have time for—'

'Springwater merchants always hold a sidewalk sale on the last Thursday of June,' Noah felt compelled to mention. 'Everyone clears out their stock to make room for their fall shipments. It's usually very successful at drawing people into town, which is why the Chamber of Commerce turned it into an annual event.'

Carrie clapped her hands. 'It'll be perfect. Can we do it, Jenny? Please? Can we? Can we? I'd rather find a good home for things like the music box than to just throw them away. It'll be good for the environment, 'cause we're recycling.'

The moment Jenny's eyes twinkled, Noah knew they had won the battle. 'OK,' she said. 'But you're in charge of it.'

Noah made an instant decision. 'And I'll help.'

Carrie's grin widened. 'Really? Promise?'

'I promise.'

Wearing a smile of victory, Carrie carefully cradled the ballerina as she skipped away. Jenny's expression hardened. 'We'll manage by ourselves,' she said stiffly.

'I'm sure you can, but I've given my word so I will.'

She visibly bristled and her blue-gray eyes flashed with fire. 'If you're insinuating that you keep your promises and I don't...'

He'd obviously touched a sore spot. 'I'm not,' he said honestly. 'It never entered my mind. I offered because I want to. That's all. No ulterior motive. Scout's honor.' He held up three fingers in the traditional salute.

She didn't appear convinced and he thought it time to

discuss something less volatile. 'It's nice of you to look after your friend's daughter. Not many people would take on the responsibility.'

'Susan's helped me many times and I wanted to return the favor. She's widowed and doesn't have any close family.'

'I assume Carrie is one of the commitments you mentioned having back in Grand Junction?'

'Look,' she said brusquely, clearly evading his question, 'I thought you came by to sort out rumors, not to discuss my friends or my personal life.'

'Sorry,' he said, not feeling sorry at all. 'I was just making conversation. But to get back on track, we were talking about you taking on a partner to ease your cash-flow problem.'

'Thanks, but no, thanks. I shared that position with my aunt and I don't care to repeat the experience. I'll manage.'

'Who said it would be the same with someone else?'

'Who said it wouldn't?' she countered.

Her mind was obviously made up, her decision irrevocable, so he dropped the subject. 'If you're leaving in the fall, are you still planning to sell?'

'Yes.'

'And what happens if you don't find a buyer?'

She straightened and hugged her arms to her chest. 'I've talked to a fellow who's interested in working here, but he's committed elsewhere until September. So I'll wait and see what develops.'

'Good luck.'

Her gaze held the same confused wariness as a doe caught in the headlights of a car. 'After last week I would have said that you would be the last person in Springwater to offer me luck. Why the change of heart?'

'Jenny?' Carrie called. 'Are you about done visiting? I'm worried about Bugs.'

'OK, squirt. Give me another minute.' She faced him. 'You were saying?' she prompted.

He asked a question of his own. 'Bugs as in insects or Bugs as in—'

Jennifer smiled. 'Bunny. Carrie's very protective of him, especially since he's in new surroundings.'

'I see.' He didn't have to stretch his imagination to visualize the little girl with a fluffy white rabbit in her arms.

'You were about to tell me why you had a change of heart,' she prompted.

'Does it matter?' he asked, relying on the same excuse she'd given him earlier. In actuality, he wasn't sure of how to answer. She certainly had reason to maintain her distance because he'd done the same from the moment she'd arrived at Earl's bedside. If he explained how Harriet's hints and the conversation he'd overheard only moments ago had softened his attitude, she'd accuse him of showing pity.

Jennifer Ruscoe wasn't a woman who would have appreciated being pitied. It was better not to say anything. For now.

'I suppose it doesn't,' she said slowly.

'It won't help either of us if people think we can't get along,' he pointed out. 'Wouldn't it serve our best interests if we started over, so to speak?'

She met his gaze squarely. 'Is it possible?'

'We can try.' If Earl hadn't resented her absences, then he shouldn't either, even if those events had brought back painful memories.

The breath she drew seemed to carry a resigned note. 'I suppose.'

Noah bent down to pick up her sign. As he handed it to her, he said with a smile, 'You'd better hang this so you can hurry home to Bugs and feed your assistant. Do you need any help?'

She shook her head. 'I can do it.'

He hadn't expected her to say otherwise, but he'd wanted to offer. 'Have a nice evening.'

He left as quietly as he'd come, aware of Jenny's mystified stare boring into his back. A hundred and one unanswered questions still burned inside him and he didn't want to say goodbye. Yet he couldn't press his luck, either. Pushing too hard, too soon, that would do more harm than good. She'd accepted a truce, and though the grounds were shaky at least it was a start.

He would have to train himself to call her 'Jenny' like everyone else, although for some strange reason it didn't seem as difficult as he'd once thought.

Last week, his only concern had been in having the pharmacy open for his patients' convenience. Now, that desire no longer seemed enough. He wanted something else, although he hadn't quite defined what it was.

He disliked leaving things undone, so perhaps his lack of answers had triggered his sense of restlessness. He understood more than he had before he'd arrived, but his curiosity hadn't been completely satisfied.

*Show her you're not the enemy.*

He'd taken the first step toward following Harriet's advice. Leaving Jenny to her own devices for the past month, that had been a mistake he wasn't going to repeat. She had clearly made big plans in the last week, and he wanted to personally watch her achieve them. Being underfoot was one way to ensure that she didn't say one thing and do another. He had a responsibility to his patients and he wouldn't shirk his duty.

It would definitely be an interesting summer.

It was going to be a long summer, Jenny thought to herself as she taped her new poster in the store's plate-glass window. She wasn't used to living in the proverbial goldfish bowl, where every move she made was dissected and analyzed. After having Noah Kimball avoid her for the past month, the possibility of seeing him on a regular basis troubled her to a certain degree.

It wasn't as if he had to say the right words or demonstrate a certain amount of friendliness to entice her to stay. She'd practically guaranteed that his precious pharmacy would be here, one way or another, just like he wanted. However, if he wanted to keep tabs on her, by generously offering his time and strong back, she wasn't going to refuse. The sooner she whipped this place into shape, the sooner she could return to Grand Junction.

She stepped back, flexing the ache out of her shoulder blades. He was right in one respect—bickering wouldn't be good for business. Although he'd implied it would hurt both of them, she would be the one to suffer. He also had more power to make her life miserable than vice versa.

In any case, her needs were too great to hold a grudge. Whether or not he actually would follow through on his word still remained to be seen.

'That's it,' she told Carrie. 'Let's eat.'

'My stomach's hungry for pizza,' Carrie said.

'Mine, too.' After shutting off all the lights except one in the rear of the building, Jenny turned the thermostat up a few degrees, then locked the door behind them.

Much later, after Bugs had eaten and they had dined on their take-out pizza from the local Pizza Hut, Carrie's eyelids started to droop.

'Are you tired, squirt?' Jenny asked as she cleared away

the remnants of their meal, certain Carrie would deny the slightest suggestion.

'Oh, no.' Carrie stifled a yawn. 'My mom lets me stay up late during the summer. Want to play Monopoly? Or how about Life?'

Jenny smiled at Carrie's choices as she ushered her upstairs to the tub. Each of those two games took hours to play before a winner could be declared. 'I'm going to pass tonight. We had a busy day and tomorrow will be the same. If I don't go to sleep soon, I won't be ready to start early in the morning. We open at eleven, so I want to get as much done as possible before customers start coming.'

'Then I can't stay up late and watch TV?'

Carrie's usually bright brown eyes had dulled. She would probably fall asleep before the ten o'clock news came on, but Jenny decided not to argue. This wasn't a battle worth fighting. 'Sure you can. Just be sure you shut off all the lights when you go to bed.'

'OK.'

Later, during Jenny's turn for a soak in the claw-footed bathtub, she heard Carrie's giggle drift up the stairs.

It reminded her of the times when she and her uncle had watched comedies together with the volume turned low in deference to Eunice sleeping across the hall. The antics of Jackie Gleason and Bob Hope had always made them laugh and they'd struggled at times not to wake her.

She sank lower in the water until the raspberry-scented bubbles tickled her chin. Leaning her head against the rim, she closed her eyes and waited for the water to soothe away the day's tensions. Life had certainly become more complicated than the old television shows had portrayed. People weren't as open and forthright either.

Noah Kimball was a perfect example. The man possessed more layers to his personality than a head of iceberg lettuce. For someone who supposedly was only concerned about having an operational pharmacy, he'd taken a more active interest in her activities than she'd expected.

Did he suspect there was more to her vague excuse for changing professions?

She dismissed the idea before it took hold. Magazines were full of stories about people who'd changed their career direction because they grew tired of their stressful lifestyles. And while the stress hadn't been the sole reason for her decision, it had played a role.

In the meantime, she'd do what had to be done in order to repay her emotional debt and make amends for her past mistakes. Once the summer ended, she would return to her teaching position and embrace her new career with a clear conscience.

Nothing would change her mind.

Over the next few days, however, she realized the monumental size of the goal she'd set for herself. The repairmen she'd hired turned the place upside down as they tackled their jobs with enthusiasm and skill. She spent hours on the phone with her suppliers, working out delivery schedules and fees. Carrie sorted through the general supplies as Jenny refilled prescriptions and studied her records to get a feel for the quantities she should stock.

Because her inventory of digoxin, a heart medication, was low, she jotted it on her list. Yet, after checking the past quarter's invoices, their pharmacy had dispensed an excessive amount for a population this size. Springwater had a small nursing home, but even if she took the geriatric population into consideration the quantities seemed extreme.

On the other hand, her uncle—and Herb—had ordered the tablets consistently each month, indicating that this wasn't a fluke. Out of curiosity, she skimmed through her prescription file, but found very few actual orders.

Where had all the tablets gone? Had Earl loaned them to another pharmacy? If so, why would he have done that on a regular basis?

Puzzled and unable to explain the discrepancy, she pushed the episode out of her mind until Wednesday's discovery of a similar problem involving vials of insulin.

At first she blamed a clerical error. However, she knew of her uncle's attention to detail and couldn't imagine him misplacing any of his inventory. Earl had controlled every aspect of his pharmacy and he'd never have delegated anything remotely connected to his bookkeeping duties.

Again, she might have dismissed her findings, except for the fact that she now had two instances of misplaced medications.

Her uncle had always been healthy, but maybe he'd been taking the medication himself. Heart disease and diabetes weren't rare conditions, although to her knowledge those diseases weren't part of her family history. Even so, if those tablets had been for personal use, she'd find a prescription.

She thumbed through the file and came up empty-handed. On impulse, she checked for Herb's name, but didn't find any records for him either.

Her uncle couldn't have taken those pills. For one thing, the amount lost exceeded any amount he might have used. For another, if he'd needed the drug, he wouldn't have played aggressive basketball with Noah and his cronies.

Jenny glanced around the area where they'd stored the pharmaceuticals since the store had first opened. The security was far from perfect. Other than a barred window, one door and one lock stood between her and the outside. A person with the right tools could have walked in and helped themselves to literally anything.

She'd already inventoried the Schedule II drugs and

could account for every tablet of Demerol, Ritalin and Percodan, to name a few. Why a thief would take legend drugs—those coming in bottles with the caption stating 'Caution: Federal law prohibits dispensing without a prescription'—instead of addictive controlled substances didn't make sense.

Instantly, she chided herself for not upgrading her security after Herb had left. She didn't suspect him of wrongdoing, but replacing the locks was a prudent defense against an extra set of keys floating around in the community.

Her analytical nature wanted answers, but the time required to review every record was a luxury she couldn't afford. Until she could manage an audit, she'd use the invoices as a guide, listen to her instincts, and stay alert for anything out of the ordinary. By next month she'd have her own facts and figures for comparison.

She could always ask Herb for an explanation, but he'd ground her pride into the dust when he'd resigned—she'd contact him only as a last resort.

Lost in her thoughts, the carpenters' steady hammering and all else faded into the background. Her customer knocked on the window-ledge near her desk to grab her attention.

Embarrassed by her daydreaming, she rose at the sight of Terrell Hawver. 'Sorry to keep you waiting. Don't tell me,' she joked to hide her sudden trepidation, 'there's a problem with my aunt.'

Terrell, a stocky man in his mid-thirties, smiled. He always wore a somewhat rumpled suit and tie, no matter what the weather. His light brown hair usually appeared as if he'd run his hands through it haphazardly and he gave the overall impression of being somewhat absentminded. Still, he'd been her uncle's attorney, and if Terrell had satisfied Earl, Jenny wouldn't complain.

'Not to my knowledge,' he said.

Watching him rub his breastbone, Jenny realized her error. 'Sorry,' she said. 'My aunt is hard to deal with and, quite frankly, I'm still amazed by how smoothly everything went.'

'Perfectly understandable. Eunice is the type of person who keeps lawyers on their toes. I'm here to ask you for advice.'

'What can I help you with?'

Once again he rubbed his chest. 'I need relief from my indigestion. Antacids help, but they don't totally relieve the symptoms. What do you suggest I use?'

'Do certain foods bother you more than others?'

'The spicier the better, but the agony afterwards outweighs the pleasure. My wife and I entertain a lot at the country club, and now I can't drink anything alcoholic without paying the price. Coffee bothers me, too.'

'Have you had a recent physical?' she asked.

'A couple of years ago.' He frowned. 'Do you think I need another one?'

'It might not hurt,' she said, considering the possibility of a duodenal ulcer. 'Have you had other problems?'

'Like what?'

'Vomiting blood, weight loss or weight gain—that sort of thing.'

He patted his pudgy stomach and grinned. 'My wife's pushing me to lose a few pounds. I guess I got in the habit of eating because it made the pain go away,' he said sheepishly. 'Between cutting the serving sizes and eating all this rabbit food, my stomach is constantly in an uproar.'

Jenny came through the half-door, skirted the sawhorses bearing pieces of plywood, and headed for her display of non-prescription stomach remedies. 'I have a few suggestions, but serving sizes are out of my control, I'm afraid,' she teased.

He grinned. 'You can't give me a note saying that I need more food with my meals? I'm shocked.'

She laughed with him at his joke. 'Sorry. I can only help with the acid problem.' Scanning the shelves, she pointed to several boxes. 'I have three different products you might try.'

He eyed his choices. 'Which one do you recommend?'

'They're all good. I'd suggest you start with this,' she said, handing him a box of famotidine. 'If it helps, then keep taking it. If not, change to one of the other brands.'

'How soon will I notice a difference?'

'It takes a while. About thirty to sixty minutes.'

He glanced at the shelf. 'Do the others work faster?'

'No,' she said. 'The trick is to find the one that works for you.'

'OK. I'll start with this.'

'The directions are on the outside,' she told him. 'Chew one tablet as soon as your symptoms develop. If you're going to eat something that you know irritates you—spicy food, for example—then chew a tablet and drink a glass of water an hour before your meal.'

'Sounds simple. I hope it works.'

'Don't take more than two every twenty-four hours,' she cautioned. 'If you need more to control your symptoms, then we should look at other options.'

'Fair enough.'

'Naturally, if you would happen to start vomiting blood, go to your doctor right away. Do you see Dr Kimball or Dr Ingram?'

'Doc Ingram has looked after my family for years. I dread the day he retires. Which, considering he's in his early sixties, probably won't be too far down the road.'

'I'm sure there's enough work for two physicians.'

'Absolutely. I hear Noah's been talking to the medical schools, trying to find someone who's interested in taking over, so I'm not worried about going without a doctor. Noah won't rest until he brings someone on board. He's done a lot for this town, you know.'

'No, I didn't.'

'Oh, my, yes. He's a real mover and a shaker. The best thing we ever did was invite him here. If there's a problem, Noah will fix it,' he finished proudly.

'How nice,' she said, making a point of acting suitably impressed.

'There's nothing the folks around here wouldn't do for him,' he added as he pulled out his billfold and removed a bill. 'It was the same way with your uncle. He's sorely missed.'

A lump suddenly formed in her throat. 'Thanks,' she murmured, handing him his change. She understood how her uncle had earned everyone's high opinion, but wondered how Noah had achieved the same status in the few short years he'd been here.

Then again, the polite and personable Dr Kimball who'd dropped by several days ago could easily have won the community's adorations in record time. If her own recent history with him hadn't been so volatile, she'd have fallen for his charms immediately and without question, too. In fact, if he kept acting this way, she'd be hard-pressed to maintain her emotional distance, but she would. She must.

It doesn't matter how well the folks in Springwater like him, she told herself in the next breath. He may have extended an olive branch so they could associate in peace, but olive branches often had strings attached. She'd been tangled once before and wouldn't fall into the same trap.

Noah would have to live with one less member in his fan club before she left at the end of the summer.

# CHAPTER FIVE

FOR the next ten days, Jenny anxiously waited for her construction projects to end. The carpenter and his crew, the electrician and his apprentice, and a steady flow of customers had been underfoot the entire time. She'd expected Noah to call or come by at least once during that time to at least check on her progress, and she'd felt a strange but keen sense of disappointment by his absence and clear lack of interest.

She hadn't accomplished as much as she would have liked in the interim, but Friday and five o'clock had finally arrived, which meant the various laborers would wrap up their respective jobs, if they hadn't already done so. Eager to start her phase of the project, she didn't waste any time locking the front door to the public.

While Carrie emptied the partially bare shelves of their merchandise, Jenny pushed her way through the boxes stacked in her storage room to reach the mop bucket and her cleaning supplies. Restoring the interior to a pristine condition ranked highest on her list of priorities.

As she backed out of the space, clutching her equipment, the tools jangling on the electrician's belt signalled his approach. She dropped her load near the doorway before she faced him.

'All done,' Gib told her, his teeth showing white through his full beard. He was a burly man in his thirties who wore a faded and sweat-stained baseball cap emblazoned with GIB'S ELECTRIC. He didn't say much while he

72

worked, which explained why he had a reputation of getting the job done in the shortest time possible.

'I'm so glad.'

He lifted off his ball cap to scratch his head with large, grease-stained fingers, revealing hair as thick and dark as the hair on his face. 'It's a good thing you had the place rewired,' he said as he resettled his cap. 'If you'd ignored it for much longer you would have had to call the fire department instead of an electrician.'

Thinking of the sparks she'd seen, she mentally patted herself on the back for spending the money now, rather than later. 'That bad?'

'You betcha. See here?' He pulled a strand of wire out of his pocket and pointed to areas along its entire length where the insulation had worn thin. 'Nearly all of the lines looked like this. You were living on borrowed time.'

She studied his example. Even to her untrained eye, the damage was obvious, and she shuddered at the idea of everything going up in smoke.

'Yup. That's what happened to the Elks Club a few years back. About two a.m. one Sunday morning. By the time we got there, the flames were shooting through the roof. After that, Earl talked about redoing this place, but he never got around to it.

'Anyway,' he continued, 'you're in tiptop condition now. You can plug in all the computers and electrical gadgetry you want to.'

'Thanks.'

He tugged on the brim of his cap, then left with his gangly assistant.

'OK, Carrie,' Jenny told the little girl, 'let's go home and change clothes before we come back and get *really* dirty.'

'Can I bring Bugs with us? He won't be in the way. He can stay in an empty box over in the corner.'

'I'm not sure all this dust will be good for him,' Jenny cautioned, not convinced that Carrie's pet was as well behaved as she claimed. An ornery rabbit could disappear for days, even weeks, in all the nooks, crannies, and other potential hiding places to be found. She didn't relish the idea of going on a lengthy search and rescue mission.

Carrie swiped the top of an empty shelf with her index finger, then held it up to show the white sawdust she'd collected. 'It's dirty, but he lives outside so he's used to dirt.'

Jenny couldn't fault her logic.

'And if he stays over in the corner,' Carrie continued, 'I can visit him every so often. He's getting lonely, 'cause I've been gone all day.'

Her tone of voice and the plea in her eyes were more than Jenny could handle. 'OK, but you have to make sure he doesn't jump out of his box. We might not find him for a long time.'

Carrie's expression brightened. 'I promise.'

They returned thirty minutes later to park in the paved alley behind the building, and found Noah leaning against the driver's side of his Blazer. She felt self-conscious in her red knit shorts, which had shrunk after years of hard washing, a multicolored plaid shirt that tied at her midriff and was liberally splattered with paint, and her grungy yet comfortable Reeboks.

As she slid out from behind the wheel of her subcompact car, he straightened and flashed a disarming smile.

His grin did funny things to her insides. If she didn't know better, she'd almost think she'd missed him. It was a crazy thought considering how she'd best describe their conversations as arguments. 'Let me guess. You've heard more rumors and dropped by to separate fact from fiction again.'

He adjusted his glasses on his nose. 'No. I'm here, as promised.'

She frowned. The only promise she recalled was the one he'd made to Carrie concering the garage sale. 'Oh?'

He nodded, extending his arms out from his sides. 'I dressed for the occasion. I'm prepared for anything.'

Jenny looked him over from head to toe. A white T-shirt depicting an orange-colored basketball and the faded black Springwater Hornets logo covered his chest. The shirt had obviously seen better days because several finger-sized holes along the shoulder and side seams revealed smooth, suntanned skin.

His athletic shorts were gray and somewhat ragged-looking and matched his Nikes which had been white at some point in the distant past. His legs appeared as strong as tree trunks and as tanned as his arms, which was surprising for a man with an indoor occupation. Then again, her uncle had once mentioned Noah's love for the outdoors.

Even in old clothes, the man was breathtakingly male. Thank heavens Carrie was only ten and immune to his physical charms. As for herself, she'd be wise to assign him a job off in a corner all by himself.

'Anything?' she clarified.

'Anything,' he reaffirmed.

She shoved her key into the newly installed door lock. 'You've just made a dangerous offer.'

'Yeah.' Carrie joined them, holding her black and white rabbit against her chest. One arm supported his hindquarters and her other hand rested across his back. 'Jenny might have you clean the basement 'cause she's scared to go down there.'

Jenny lifted her chin as she shoved the door open. 'I'm *not* scared. I'm just not particularly fond of spiders and other many-legged creatures.'

'When it's time to tackle the basement, I'll volunteer,' Noah said.

'I'll go with you,' Carrie said. 'I don't mind bugs either.'

'If the boss sends us to the dungeon, I'll welcome your company,' he told the little girl somberly. 'So this is the famous Bugs. What breed is he?'

Carrie beamed with pride. 'See how his front half is white and the back half is colored? That means he's Dutch. I've had him since he was a baby.'

'That long?'

She nodded. 'I'm trying to teach him some tricks, but he's not co-operating.'

'What can rabbits do?' he asked, crouching down to her eye level.

'They can't do too many things, 'cause they're not smart like dogs or cats. Bugs will walk on a lead rope, but that's all. Now, my friend Laurie has a rabbit and he can do neat tricks.'

'Like what?' he asked.

'Jump fences. Bugs has done it a few times, but he won't very often. I think he's scared. Mom says he's just lazy. Go ahead and pet him,' she urged. 'He likes to have his forehead rubbed.'

Noah's long, lean fingers stroked the white blaze extending down Bugs's black face. Jenny saw the bunny's nose twitch and his eyes close, as if savoring the moment. She wondered how many women had enjoyed the same experience. With Noah's looks and the mystique of his profession, females probably fell at his feet on a regular basis.

She, however, wouldn't be one of them.

'If you guys are through visiting, we can get started,' Jenny said, pointedly motioning to the open door.

Noah winked at Carrie. 'Is she always such a slave-driver?'

Carrie giggled as she stepped over the threshold. 'Only when she's anxious to get something done. She pays good, though.'

Noah waited for Jenny to pass before he followed and closed the door. 'No kidding? What's the going rate these days?'

Carrie walked over to the waiting area and the large box she'd commandeered earlier. Holding Bugs by the scruff of his neck and supporting his hindquarters with her other hand, she carefully lowered her pet inside.

'I get five dollars a day plus she orders pizza every time I want it. I've got plenty saved up to go to the movies and for trips to the pool. If you do a good job, she'll pay you, too. Whatever you want.'

'Well, now,' he drawled, his eyes sparkling with an unholy gleam, 'I'm sure I can think of an appropriate form of compensation.'

Certain that his payment suggestion wasn't a suitable topic for an impressionable young mind, Jenny inter-rupted, 'Carrie? Why don't you see if you can find some-thing to hold water for Bugs?'

Once Carrie had hurried out of earshot, Jenny turned on him. 'Don't get your hopes up, Romeo,' she warned. 'I'm not that kind of girl.'

He pressed a hand against his chest and grinned. 'You're the one who jumped to the wrong conclusions. I didn't say a word.'

'I saw the gleam in your eye. Don't deny it.'

'I won't, but it must have been on your mind, too, or you wouldn't have considered the possibility either.'

Her face warmed at his accuracy. Luckily, Carrie returned with a small plastic bowl filled with water and Jenny shot him a warning glare before she became all business. 'As you can see, the place needs a thorough cleaning. After that, we need to assemble my new shelving units.'

Noah's gaze slowly raked across the room and she tried to see the changes from his perspective. Just glancing around the room, it gave her a feeling of pride in what had already been accomplished.

The latest style in decorator plywood covered the walls. Stripping off the old wallpaper, it had literally been more trouble than it had been worth because of layers plastered over layers. To create the same overall effect, she and Carrie had chosen a pattern of faint blue stripes on a white background.

Mike, the carpenter, had replaced the ceiling tiles and Gib had converted the old fluorescent light fixtures to a more modern recessed version. Unfortunately, the new flooring would have to wait until she had the money to pay the carpetlayer. She would have preferred having her projects done all at once, but she could only afford to do a little at a time. Already in hock up to her eyebrows, she didn't want to dig her financial hole any deeper than it already was.

'It looks great. Really great,' he commented at last. 'You've been putting in long hours to have accomplished so much in such a short time.'

She relaxed under his praise. 'We have worked hard, haven't we, Carrie?'

'Yeah,' the little girl piped in. 'We've worked so hard, we haven't had time to go swimming.'

'Next week,' Jenny promised.

He pivoted full circle to study his surroundings. 'No one can accuse you of not being committed to your venture.'

Considering the money she'd spent lately, her commitment was far greater than he could possibly have imagined. 'Were you afraid I wasn't?'

He paused, then had the grace to appear sheepish. 'The possibility crossed my mind.'

His doubt didn't surprise her; his honesty did. 'And now? Are you convinced?'

'Absolutely.' Sincerity rang in his voice.

She didn't particularly care one way or another about his opinion, but his endorsement could either make or break her business. 'Well, then. I hope you're ready to start.'

'Just say the word.'

Jenny took a step toward the cleaning supplies she'd laid out, but his hand snagged her arm and she stopped. 'You're not angry because I had some doubts?' His tone was cautious.

'I asked for the truth and you gave it to me. If I don't like to hear it, it's my problem, not yours.' She felt a smile tugging at the corners of her mouth. 'Besides, I'd rather get even.'

He raised one eyebrow. 'Get even?'

'That's right. You get to scrub the floor.'

'Scrub the floor.'

'You volunteered to help with anything,' she reminded him, delighting in his momentary surprise.

'I might have known,' he grumbled without rancor. 'I suppose I have to get down on my hands and knees.'

She grinned, curious to see how far she could push before he'd retract his offer. 'Is there any other way?'

He groaned, then sighed. 'Would it do any good to tell you about my football injury?'

Jenny glanced at his legs. Neither had any surgical scars marring the skin and, in fact, looked perfect. 'Football?'

'No, but it sounded good.' His disarming smile tugged at her heart and she took pity on him.

'Actually, I have a mop you can use.'

His face brightened. 'Wonderful. Where's it at?'

'Coming right up.' On her way to the corner, where she'd laid out her cleaning equipment, she heard a scratching noise coming from Bugs's box. Suspicious, she detoured to investigate.

Bugs was waddling around his makeshift cage as if searching for something. 'Carrie?' Jenny called. 'Are you sure Bugs can't jump out?'

Both Carrie and Noah joined her to peer down at the rabbit who, as if realizing he'd attracted an audience, overturned his water bowl.

Carrie retrieved the container from under his foot. 'I thought he might tip over the dish because it's so light. I should have brought his special bottle.'

'There's a small metal mixing bowl under the sink,' Jenny recalled. 'Try that. If he knocks it over, he'll just have to go without until he gets home.'

'OK.' Carrie scratched his forehead. 'You'll be a good boy, won't you, Bugs?'

The rabbit rubbed his chin against her hand in contentment, and a few minutes later she scampered off to find the dish.

Noah's gaze followed her as she disappeared from view. 'She's a cute kid. Has she found any playmates yet?'

'We haven't had time.' Jenny ignored her twinge of guilt for keeping Carrie too busy to enjoy her vacation. 'Next week, I'm going to call an old friend of mine who has a daughter about her age. I also called the Recreation Center last Monday and enrolled her in a few of their summer art classes. Contrary to what you might think, I'm not working her from sunup to sundown.'

A teasing light showed in his dark eyes. 'What a relief. I'd hate to see our only pharmacist in jail for abusing the child labor laws.'

She grinned. 'So would I.'

'What did you say her mother was doing this summer?'

'Susan is working on her master's degree research project, studying some animal to see if it should be added to the endangered species list. I don't know the specifics, other than she has to camp in a fairly remote area.'

'Sounds interesting.'

'It does,' she agreed. 'Except for the camping part. I don't mind roughing it for a few days, but not for weeks on end.'

'A kindred spirit,' he drawled. 'Your uncle loved to go on extended fishing trips. I went with him a few times, but I was always more than ready to fall into a decent bed after a couple of nights.'

The talk about beds elicited an image of him sprawled across the length of the mattress with his hair tousled and his face shadowed in dark whiskers. The glimmer in his eyes suggested that he was suffering from the same problem in reverse.

Luckily, Carrie returned and diverted Jenny's wayward thoughts. 'It was right where you said it was,' she said as she placed the bowl in the box's wet corner. The rabbit opened his eyes at the sound of her voice, then closed them again.

Appeased by Bugs's apparent adjustment to his temporary quarters, Jenny pointed toward the main window. 'We'll start in the front and work our way to the back. Is that OK with you?'

Noah gave her a snappy salute. 'Aye, aye, skipper. All hands accounted for and ready to swab the deck.'

Carrie giggled. 'You're funny for a doctor.'

He winked at her. 'We'd better get to work before Jenny makes us walk the plank.' He grabbed a broom and headed for the front of the store, shortening his steps so Carrie could keep up.

Jenny watched Noah give Carrie his undivided attention as the child chattered away. His charm was definitely at work—the same charm that caused everyone in town to hold him in such high regard.

He turned suddenly. 'Do you want to move these old shelves first?' A wide grin spread across his face as he caught her staring at him like a love-struck teenager.

'Good idea.' Embarrassed, she avoided his gaze as she hurried forward and grabbed one end of the long wooden shelving unit. 'Are you ready?'

He raised one eyebrow. 'These look heavy. Maybe we should call someone to help—'

'Take care of your end and I'll take care of mine,' she retorted.

He shook the rickety structure. 'Are you going to keep these?'

'No.'

'It would be easier to break them down first.'

'All right. I'll get my tools.'

Before long, they'd reduced all the shelves to a pile of scrap lumber.

'I'll assemble the new ones,' he offered.

She shook her head. 'Sorry, bud. If you think you can get out of swabbie detail this easy, you can think again. I'm pretty good with a hammer myself.'

He snapped his fingers. 'Just my luck!'

'While you're scrubbing, I'll haul what's left out to the dumpster,' she decided.

'I'll take care of it since I'm waiting for Carrie to finish sweeping.'

'I'm capable of carrying boards,' she said firmly. 'I wouldn't want to deprive you of your own fun.'

'Spoilsport.'

She grinned. 'I know. Once you prove how handy you are with a mop, I'll promote you to assistant carpenter.'

'Fair enough.' He dunked the sponge head into the bucket of soapy water, before running it across the tile. 'You're enjoying this, aren't you?'

Jenny watched his shirt strain across his back as he washed Carrie's freshly swept floor. If he only knew... 'You bet,' she said. 'It's the first time I've ever had a doctor at my mercy. Maybe I should snap a photo to document the occasion.'

He cast an innocent look in her direction. 'Don't forget. Paybacks can be hell.'

'I'm quaking in my boots. By the way, you'd better hurry up, or you won't be finished in time to get a cone before the Ice Cream Churn closes.'

He rinsed the mop and cleaned another section. 'So you're paying in ice cream tonight?'

'That's right.'

Noah glanced at Carrie who was looking on with interest. 'Is that OK with you?' At her nod, he said, 'Then it's OK with me. The grunts have to stand together, don't we, short stuff?'

Carrie giggled. 'I'm not short.'

He appeared to give the matter some thought. 'You're not?'

She shook her head, her ponytail swaying like the pendulum of a grandfather clock. 'You're just tall.'

Leaving the two behind to carry on their own conversation, Jenny carried the broken pieces of shelving outside, then slipped away to the corner of the pharmacy that served as her office. She needed to place another order, but before she did she wanted to check some of the old invoices so as not to miss anything.

Nothing seemed out of the ordinary, until she ran across several large purchases of fluconazole tablets. Used for a variety of yeast and fungal infections, she wasn't surprised to find it listed on an invoice.

Yet not a single bottle graced her shelves.

She tapped her pencil against her temple, trying to remember if she'd ever seen a record of the drug being dispensed. If only her uncle had taken the plunge and entered the computer age her task would be so much easier.

In the end, she decided to order only a small supply. It was too expensive to sit on the shelf and tie up her inventory dollars for an indefinite period. If someone needed it, she'd have enough to start their treatment regimen. Her supplier could overnight express the rest.

Noah poked his head through the window. 'We're all done. How are you coming in here?'

'Fine.' She toyed with the idea of asking Noah about the medication. Being one of the town's two physicians, the chances of an affected patient being his were fifty per cent. And even if the case wasn't his, he'd know about it from an infection control standpoint.

He might hesitate to answer her questions on the grounds of breaking confidentiality, but she wasn't asking for names. The drugs she hadn't been able to account for in recent days could easily have caused the drain on the pharmacy's finances and literally threatened its existence.

That reason alone should encourage him to co-operate.

On the other hand, she felt uneasy about discussing the situation. Perhaps she was looking for a problem where none existed. And even if it *did* turn out to be an issue, she didn't want to mention it to a man who, for all intents and purposes, was still a stranger.

But what difference would her investigation make? a little voice argued. The money and pharmaceuticals were long gone—she wouldn't recoup those losses at this late date. It was time to start over.

His smile turned to a frown. 'What's wrong?'

She quickly marshalled her thoughts as she rose. Maybe she'd satisfy her curiosity some other time, but not now. After all, the puzzle was hers to solve, not his. 'Sorry. My mind was someplace else. We'll build two of the new units—it shouldn't take too long because they're in kits—then call it a night.'

'Do you want them in the same arrangement as the old ones?' he asked.

She rejoined him as she answered. 'No. I want to see everyone who walks in and I can't do that with a lot of clutter in the middle of the room.'

Since she only had one set of tools, Noah organized an assembly line. Carrie acted as assistant, handing over crucial screws and tools like a well-trained surgical nurse. Because Jenny didn't own a power screwdriver, fastening the pieces together took time and a lot of muscle. In the end, they both took turns spelling each other.

Because their system was efficient they finished sooner than Jenny had originally thought, and she decided to assemble the remaining two storage units. Before long, everything stood in place and appeared exactly the way she'd envisioned.

'The center looks awfully bare,' he commented.

'It won't be for long,' she said. 'I'm displaying my new products there.'

'What do you have in mind?'

'Nutritional and vitamin supplements. Some herbal products, too.'

'Sounds like you'll need the shelves we tore apart.'

She grinned. 'I'm going to use some of the old cabinets and tables that are stored in the basement. They're real character pieces.'

'You've given this a lot of thought, haven't you?'

'Just trying to make every penny stretch.' She turned to Carrie. 'Are you ready for ice cream?'

'Yippee. I'm ready. I'll get Bugs.'

Since Jenny's house was on the way to the Ice Cream Churn, Noah followed her home where they dropped Bugs off to enjoy his own rabbit treats. As soon as Carrie had secured him in his hutch, they piled into Noah's Blazer to travel on to their destination.

Surprisingly, as it was eight o'clock, they had the place all to themselves.

'Enjoy the peace and quiet now. We'll be busy by eight-thirty,' the girl in the pink uniform said in answer to Jenny's question. 'The softball and baseball games start ending around then.'

After ordering Carrie's Rocky Road waffle cone, Noah's chocolate chip, and her own strawberry cheesecake, Jenny led the way to a booth in a far corner.

Although Carrie sat beside Jenny, Jenny was extremely conscious of Noah across the short table. Occasionally, their knees brushed together by accident and, flustered by the sudden heat, she nearly licked the top scoop of strawberry cheesecake ice cream right off her cone.

'Was this place here when you were a little girl?' Carrie asked, catching the drips with her tongue.

'No, it wasn't,' Jenny said. 'We served drinks and ice cream in our store.'

Carrie's eyes grew wide. 'You did?'

'Yes. When I wasn't stocking shelves I worked behind the counter, making banana splits, malts and floats.'

'Gee, too bad we can't do it again,' Carrie said.

'It was a lot of work. Now there are too many other restaurants in town to compete with.'

Carrie licked her cone again, smearing ice cream on her nose. 'Since we're a pharmacy, we'd better stick to what we do best.'

Noah pushed an extra napkin in Carrie's direction. 'Spoken like a savvy businesswoman. So tell me more about Bugs,' he said. 'What does he like to eat?'

With the two deep in conversation about alfalfa pellets and the ingredients of rabbit mix, Jenny's thoughts drifted back to the discrepancies she'd found. Although she'd only spot-checked a small portion of her inventory, the things she'd encountered so far were worrisome. All indications suggested that her uncle had lost a great deal of money in recent months, if not years.

On the other hand, she had good news. With both Herb and Earl gone, any problems had basically resolved themselves. Becoming financially solvent no longer seemed impossible.

Carrie nudged her. 'Can you let me out? I want to wash my hands.'

'Oh, sure.' Jenny moved so Carrie could scoot past her and head for the bathroom.

Noah leaned back. 'You're preoccupied this evening.'

She pleated the extra, unused napkin. 'I suppose I am.'

'Want to talk about whatever's bothering you?'

'Not really.' *Go ahead*, a little voice urged. Acting on impulse, she asked, 'You were Uncle Earl's doctor, weren't you?'

'Yes. After Dr Ingram suffered a mild heart attack and brought me on board, Earl started coming to see me. Why?'

She posed another question, instead of answering his. 'Had he been sick before the accident?'

'Sick? As in…?' He waited expectantly for her to fill in the gaps.

'Was he on any maintenance medication for a chronic condition?'

'I didn't prescribe any.' He leaned forward, his gaze intense. 'What are you saying?'

'So far, I've noticed discrepancies in insulin vials, digoxin tablets, and the antifungal agent, fluconazole.'

'I assume you've already ruled out a clerical error.'

She nodded.

'Are you implying that he was medicating himself?'

'I'm not implying anything, although he certainly would have known how to calculate the dosages. Even if that were the case, the numbers exceed what any one person could use during that time period.

'Also, the antifungal was received a few days before he died. If it was for his personal use, then I should still have those bottles on my shelf. If it wasn't and he'd ordered such large quantities because of an outbreak of thrush or *Cryptococcus* meningitis, I'd have a record of where those pills went. I can't find either.'

'Have you talked to Herb?'

'We talked about the ordering procedure shortly after the funeral,' she admitted. 'He knew the procedures, but Uncle Earl personally monitored his inventory. Occasionally Herb special-ordered something if Earl went on vacation, but that rarely happened. His handwriting wasn't as neat as I remembered, but I still recognized it as his.'

She paused, hating to ask her next question. 'He wasn't becoming senile, was he?'

# CHAPTER SIX

NOAH stared at Jenny as if she'd lost her mind. 'Earl? Senile? If you'd been around, you'd know…'

She winced at his cold tone. She'd made him angry and she hadn't meant to. 'If I'd been around,' she said, 'things probably would have been different. But I wasn't and I don't need any more guilt added to what I already feel. However, something strange was going on and I'm trying to explore all reasonable possibilities.'

He sat back, the angry light in his eyes dimming as he appeared somewhat appeased by her explanation. 'Earl was the sharpest man I knew. He'd been working fewer hours in order to pursue his "other interests" as he called them, but his mental faculties were very much intact.'

'It didn't seem likely,' she admitted, regretting her impulsive question and hoping the last few minutes of their evening would return to their formerly even keel. 'But I had to ask. I don't like loose ends.'

'Earl complained at times of arthritis,' Noah commented, stroking his chin thoughtfully, 'but it wasn't severe enough for anything stronger than an OTC med. It could explain the change in his handwriting.'

One mystery solved, she thought. 'Probably so.'

'I can't think of anything else off the top of my head, but if you want another detective on the case, I'm game,' he said. 'I can't break patient confidentiality, but I can help you sort through papers and piece information together.'

'Thanks, but I'll probably let the whole thing drop. The

only person with the answers isn't around to ask, so why waste any more time on speculation? Even if I found out the truth, it wouldn't change anything. The meds are gone and the money's been spent.' Jenny hated the idea of giving up her search for answers, but didn't have any choice.

'You're right,' he agreed, 'although I can understand your need to know.' A half-smile tugged at his mouth. 'By any chance, do you reconcile your banking statements down to the penny?'

The tense moment had passed. 'I shouldn't confess this, because everyone tells me I'm being ridiculous, but I do. I'll spend hours looking for any error, even if it's only a few cents.'

He grinned. 'Is it worth it?'

She laughed. 'No, but it's the principle of the matter. If it's my error, I want to know. If it's the bank's, I want them to correct it. As Ben Franklin said, 'A penny saved is a penny earned.''

'Then you're not the type of person who'll dismiss the errors you've found in your business ledgers.'

She sighed. 'Probably not. I thought if I kept telling myself to forget the past, I would. It works for a while, and then I'm afraid that whatever had caused my uncle's financial problems could also affect me.'

'Then you should keep digging.'

She thought of the boxes stored in the basement. They would either be a treasure trove or a junk pile. 'Whatever I decide to do will have to wait until I organize my own system of bookkeeping. It doesn't make sense to delve into the past if my current records are a mess.'

Carrie reappeared with clean hands at the same time as a group of twelve young boys entered, wearing dirty baseball uniforms and congratulating themselves on their win. 'I'm ready to go,' she announced.

Although Jenny had known this moment would arrive, she hated to see it come. She'd enjoyed the evening far more than she'd ever imagined. Telling herself that all good things eventually came to an end, she grabbed her bag. 'Then let's head for home.'

Noah ushered the two out to his Blazer. Carrie skipped ahead a few steps to open the doors, while Noah stayed close to Jenny's side. His hand rested on the small of her back, exerting a gentle pressure. The light touch stirred her senses and comforted her at the same time.

She'd never felt this way about Ted, which, considering he'd turned out to be on the level of pond scum, had been a blessing in disguise.

She and Ted had enjoyed some good times in the early days of their relationship. She'd been comfortable with him, but 'comfortable' didn't describe the feeling that Noah's presence evoked in her. All of her senses seemed heightened, as if something inside her had homed in on him alone.

What nonsense, she scolded herself. Ted had taught her a hard lesson about men who lived by the concept of the ends justifying the means. No matter how easily Noah made her insides quiver, she wouldn't forget what she had learned. Noah's interest lay purely in having a pharmacy in town. If he had to wine and dine the only pharmacist as part of his strategy, he would.

As he drove back to her home, Carrie stuck her head between the two front seats and stared at Jenny. 'I thought Noah did a good job with scrubbing tonight. Didn't you?'

'Yes, he did.'

'Did he do better than you thought he would?'

Pinned under Carrie's expectant gaze and Noah's questioning one, she answered, 'Yes, he did.'

Carrie nodded in apparent satisfaction. 'Then you have to pay him more than an ice-cream cone.'

'Yeah,' he chimed in. 'I deserve a bonus.'

'The deal was ice cream,' she reminded them. 'I don't remember our verbal contract including a bonus.'

'But he did a lot of work,' Carrie insisted. 'He deserves more than ice cream.'

Suspicious, Jenny narrowed her eyes as she met Noah's gaze. 'Did you put her up to this?'

'I did not. Honest,' he said, turning the corner. 'How could I? You were with us the whole time.'

'I thought of it all by myself,' Carrie said proudly. Turning her head to stare at Noah, she added, 'So, what else would you like?'

Jenny saw a familiar unholy gleam light up his eyes and braced herself.

'What I'd like,' he began slowly, 'I wouldn't get, so I'll settle for a basketball game. One on one.'

'A game?' Jenny had been certain he'd ask for something else...something more intimate...something like a kiss. In her heart, relief fought against disappointment.

He nodded. 'A game. First one to sink five baskets wins.'

The opportunity to best him dangled in front of her like a prize. His size might be to his advantage, but she'd learned a few tricks to even the odds. 'Only five? How about ten? Or twenty?'

'Five,' he insisted. 'Winner gets to ask a question and the loser has to give a straight answer.'

Suddenly wary, she asked, 'What kind of questions are we talking about?'

He shrugged. 'Anything. Everything. The sky's the limit.'

'Somehow, I'm not surprised.'

He grinned. 'I'll even share my personal stats. Height, weight, shoe size, whatever.'

'If you think I'm going to tell you *mine*, you'd better think twice.'

'Ah, but you'd have to lose first, wouldn't you?' he said smugly.

'True, but I won't.'

He raised an eyebrow. 'Then you don't have anything to worry about.'

Somehow, she felt as if she'd been hustled. 'So why play? We could just toss a coin.'

'You don't want to experience the thrill of victory and the agony of defeat?'

If he only knew. 'I just think we can compete without the question-and-answer period tied to the outcome.'

'Yeah, but when I get together with the guys, the losers always buy a beer at the pool hall.'

'I don't mind if you buy me a beer. I'm also not horrified at the prospect of going into a pool hall.'

He shook his head. 'Sorry. Different game, different stakes. Do we have a deal?'

Carrie interrupted, her eyes owlish as she followed their conversation. 'That's what you want? To play a basketball game?' She clearly thought the adults had lost their minds.

'That's what I want,' he told her.

'Jenny's going to cream you,' Carrie warned him. 'My mom says nobody at home wants to play against her any more 'cause she beats the socks off everybody.'

His eyes lit up. 'Is that like strip poker?'

Jenny shot him a look of disgust. Then, involuntarily, the mental picture he'd painted formed and an anticipatory shiver ran down her spine.

'Absolutely not,' she said firmly, forcing the image out of her mind. 'It was a figure of speech.'

Noah grinned. 'You're fun to tease, Ms Ruscoe. To answer your question, Carrie, yes, I want to challenge Jenny to a basketball game.'

Carrie shook her head slowly as she spoke. 'You don't know what you're in for.'

Jenny plunged ahead, eager to win one for her uncle. 'It's a deal. When do you want to play? Tomorrow?'

'What's wrong with right now?'

'Now?' She stared at him in stunned surprise.

'Sure, why not? It's still early. Barely nine.'

Better to meet his demand now, rather than stew about it for a few days. 'OK,' she said, her adrenalin rising at the challenge.

'Where are you going to play?' Carrie asked.

Jenny glanced at Noah. 'Our driveway?'

'Perfect. It's like my home court,' he assured her as he turned down River's End Drive and parked in front of the two-story house that had served as home to three generations of Ruscoes. 'Earl and I spent a lot of hours together here.'

Darn, she thought, opening her door to jump out. He probably knew every crack in the concrete better than she did.

'Bugs and I can referee and keep score,' Carrie offered as Noah helped her and her rabbit out of the back seat.

'Wonderful idea,' Noah answered as he rummaged through his gear and freed a pair of relatively new Nikes from his duffle bag. 'We need someone unbiased to settle any disputes.'

Carrie flashed him a grin, before hurrying toward Bugs's hutch. They had placed it between the house and the detached garage for maximum shade and protection from the near-constant wind.

'I'm not sure how unbiased she's going to be,' Jenny

muttered, aware of how Carrie had blossomed under Noah's attention. After the death of Susan's husband, males had been in short supply in their household.

Noah walked alongside Jenny up the driveway, with his shoes tied together by the laces and slung over one shoulder. 'What makes you say that?'

'She likes you,' she said simply.

His smile stretched from ear to ear. 'I think she's pretty neat myself. Don't worry, though. I'm sure Bugs will keep her from making too many prejudiced calls.'

She laughed at the idea. 'How reassuring.'

It took about ten minutes for Jenny to exchange her T-shirt and dilapidated tennis shoes for a white Colorado University tank top and a pair of running shoes. As she came outside, she caught Noah in the middle of his warm-up exercises.

'Where's Carrie?' she asked, doing a few stretches of her own.

'Looking for a whistle,' he answered.

As the sun edged toward the western horizon, she guessed they had about forty-five minutes of daylight left. Shadows shrouded parts of the driveway, so she flicked on the light over the back door and lit several potted citronella candles to ward off mosquitoes.

Moments later, Carrie arrived on the scene, testing her whistle with short, shrill bursts. 'It works,' she said cheerfully.

Jenny exchanged amused glances with Noah, wincing as Carrie once again demonstrated the whistle's ability. 'Yeah, well, use it sparingly. I'd hate to have the neighbors complain about us disturbing the peace.'

'OK. I'll be careful.' Carrie slipped the cord over her head and looked at each of them expectantly. 'Are you guys ready?'

'I think so,' Jenny declared.

'The usual boundaries?' he asked.

'Fine.' The driveway butted against the house on the right and an eight-foot-high wooden fence on the left. The backboard was bolted above the garage door and the concrete slab ran all the way to the sidewalk. The enclosed area contained most of the stray balls, but if one of the buildings or the fence were hit, possession went to the other person.

Carrie tossed the ball in the air and hurried out of the way to stand by Bugs's hutch. Noah's long arms snagged the basketball as it made its descent, but by the time he'd dribbled half-court Jenny had stolen it and sent it arching toward the hoop.

Swish. 'One for me,' she crowed.

'Lucky shot.' Noah brought the ball in from out of bounds. Once again, she wiggled in close and stole the ball. Before he could recover, she scored another basket.

'Two for me,' she said gleefully.

He stopped and held the ball under one arm. 'Are you sure she's not cheating, Carrie?'

Carrie clapped her hands and giggled. 'I told you she was good.'

It didn't take Jenny long to score two more points. The key, she'd discovered, was to work her way inside and watch for the split second when she could snatch the ball away from him.

He called time out. 'Want to go for ten points instead of five?'

Jenny grinned, her skin heated from the exertion. 'Not a chance.'

Carrie signaled the end of their break. As soon as Noah entered the court Jenny tried another steal maneuver, but failed. The ball bounced toward the sidewalk and they both ran after it. Forgetting the location of the crack and the uneven patch of concrete, Jenny stumbled. Her feet tangled with Noah's and she lost her balance.

She reached out instinctively and the next thing she knew she was safe in his embrace, pressed against his chest as he supported her weight. In that split second, she noticed a great many things.

His skin was warm and covered in a faint sheen of perspiration. His heart beat steadily under her hand, his breathing slightly labored.

Every time he exhaled, a whisper of air laced with chocolate flowed across her cheek. The fresh scent of the outdoors clung to him in a not unpleasant manner and mingled with his woodsy fragrance to create a provocative all-male aroma.

'Are you OK?' he asked, his hold on her firm.

She raised her chin to meet his gaze. His mouth hovered over hers by a few inches and was far too enticing for her peace of mind.

'Yeah.' The word came out in a whisper and she cleared her throat. 'I tripped.'

'Tricky spot,' he said, his attention focused on her lower lip.

'I should have remembered where it was,' she said, aware of how breathless she sounded.

'All's well that ends well,' he said.

Suddenly aware of his hands splayed across her back, the lack of air space between their bodies and the curiosity of an eleven-year-old bystander, Jenny pushed on his chest, vividly conscious of his pectoral muscles rippling underneath her palms as he set her on her feet.

'Yes,' she agreed. 'All's well that ends well. Thanks.'

He held her until she regained her footing, then let go with seeming reluctance. 'Any time.'

'It's Jenny's ball,' Carrie declared from the sidelines.

'My ball,' Jenny agreed. Her legs wouldn't respond to her intention to fetch the item in question from where it had rolled into the street.

Noah jogged over to its stopping point by the curb. 'Ready?' he asked, before tossing it to her.

Forcing herself to refocus as she caught the ball with both hands, she drew confidence from the feel of the familiar dimpled leather surface against her fingertips. One more basket; she only needed to sink one more basket. Then she could forget the whole episode.

Or at least, she could *try* to do so. It wouldn't be easy.

'Yeah. Sure,' she said. 'I'm ready.'

But as soon as she crossed the line and he stood his ground to block her with outstretched arms, her concentration vanished. The sight of his hands replayed the sensation of having them rest on her back. Her momentary lapse slowed her reflexes just enough for him to steal the ball and dart out of reach.

His long legs carried him toward the hoop for an easy lay-up. 'At last! I'm on the scoreboard,' he said with satisfaction.

'Only because I felt sorry for you,' she said to goad him.

'You felt sorry for me?'

'Yeah,' she said, compelled to continue her fib. It wouldn't do for him to realize that being pressed against him for those few seconds had dramatically shortened her attention span. Without a doubt, his flawless form rivaled a personal trainer's.

'For being so…so…' she thought quickly '…out of shape.'

In a split second, his attitude changed. His eyes gleamed with a competitiveness she hadn't seen before now. In a split second, it occurred to her that while he'd been playing well, he'd held part of himself back and he wouldn't continue to any longer.

His smile curved slowly until it revealed perfectly straight teeth. 'Out of shape, hmm? We'll see who's out of shape.' He leaned closer to murmur in her ear. 'For the record, I think yours is *perfect*.'

His comment totally threw her off stride. The game began again and he dogged her every step without mercy. Yet, in spite of his determination, he didn't employ the same rough tactics men often used on each other.

He didn't have to. As he guarded her with both arms outstretched, he lightly brushed any bare patch of skin within reach. Each touch, seemingly inadvertent, sent her hormones into overdrive and she fumbled the ball like a novice.

'Foul!' she called out when the score had tied at four to four and her nerves couldn't take the strain any longer. If he didn't stop, she was going to puddle on the concrete at his feet. Already, her temperature had skyrocketed to a feverish high and she was glad it had become too dark for anyone to see her flushed face. The muscles in her legs ached from the demands she'd placed on them and each breath sounded like an asthmatic wheeze. She hadn't played this intensely for a long time.

'It was not,' he protested, the glimmer of a smile showing in his eyes as if he had known how she'd respond and planned his attack accordingly.

'Hey, ref?' Jenny appealed to Carrie. 'It's a foul if the opposing player makes physical contact.'

'I was chasing away mosquitoes,' he explained, looking as innocent as he sounded.'

'I didn't feel any mosquitoes,' she answered.

'Because I chased them away before they could bite.'

'Likely story,' Jenny grumbled.

Carrie gave up her perch by the hutch to approach them. 'Did he hit you or trip you?'

'No,' Jenny admitted.

'Then it's OK.' She blew her whistle as she returned to her viewing position. 'Besides, I can't call a foul if I didn't see it. Play ball.'

'You've created a monster,' Jenny accused as she dribbled the ball with her right hand, her left arm in front of her for protection. 'A tyrant.'

He grinned. 'You can appeal to the other authority.'

She scoffed. 'Yeah, right. Like Bugs is going to stick his furry little neck out. He knows where his next meal is coming from.' Seeing an opening, she darted past him in a fast break for the hoop. Just as she was ready to shoot, Noah grabbed her from behind. With a brawny arm across her midriff, he turned her until she faced the dimly lit street.

Before she could protest, he snagged the ball, pivoted and scored his final point.

'Five to four!' Carrie called out. 'Noah won.'

'He cheated,' Jenny declared, her body on fire from his intimate hold underneath her breasts. 'You can't pick up another player and move them so you can steal the ball.'

Carrie stared at her. 'You weren't hurt, were you?'

'Well, no.'

The youngster shrugged. 'When I play with my mom, she does that, too, so it must be OK. Now, if you were hurt, that's a diff'rent story.'

Unfortunately, Jenny *was* hurting, but in places she couldn't discuss with a child, much less the man who'd caused her such discomfort.

'I demand a rematch,' Jenny insisted. She didn't intend to let Noah Kimball beat her at her own sport.

Noah stood quietly in the shadows, watching the exchange with the ball tucked under his left arm. 'I was hoping you'd say that,' he told her, pleased at the prospect of another go-round. 'Name the time and place.'

'Tomorrow. Here. Eight o'clock.'

'I wouldn't miss it for the world,' he said, amused to see her so flustered over her loss. Then again, he loved to see her with her hair all messed, her skin flushed and gleaming with a faint sheen. Whoever had originally coined the saying, 'Men sweat, women glisten,' had certainly had a way with words.

The picture she made—her breasts heaving with every breath—was marked in his memory, as was the sensation of her lithe body pressed against his. When he'd challenged her to a hoop-shooting contest, he hadn't expected it to become such an exhilarating experience. He'd need a cold shower before he'd fall asleep tonight.

'I'm going to teach Carrie the proper rules of the game before then,' she said.

'I don't know. I like her rules.' He found Jenny's discomfiture quite satisfying. He didn't feel particularly guilty over his unorthodox move, because Jenny was a formidable opponent and he'd wanted to win at any cost. Defeating her on the court was a way to get his answers.

'So, do you still think I'm out of shape?'

She grinned. 'No.' Suddenly a troubled look crossed her face. 'Go ahead. Fire away.'

Her stiff movements spoke of her dread. Clearly, she considered certain subjects taboo but, to give her credit, she hadn't limited the topics. Guessing her fear was rooted in her former job, his gut told him to tread carefully. If he dug too deep right away, he wouldn't go far with his question-answer period. He was too intrigued by Earl's niece to let impatience ruin everything.

'Are you that anxious to get rid of me?' he countered.

Once again, her skin color darkened under the glow of the overhead bulb.

'Before we get to that,' he continued smoothly, 'can you spare the winner a glass of water?'

'Of course. Come on in. Where there aren't any mosquitoes.'

He hid his smile at her pointed remark, recognizing her warning to keep his hands to himself. Not that he wouldn't with a chaperone present. He waited while Carrie crooned her goodnights to Bugs and Jenny blew out the flickering candles. Once inside, Jenny surprised him by sending Carrie to her bath.

She really was worried about something.

Noah leaned against the counter and watched Jenny wash her hands and fill two plastic tumblers with ice, then water. 'Earl always bragged on how good a ball handler you are,' he said. 'He wasn't wrong. I had to work harder than I thought I'd have to.'

She handed him a drink, then gestured toward the chairs surrounding the round kitchen table. 'That's some consolation, I suppose. You're very good, yourself. Did you play in college?'

He straddled a chair, then drank deeply until he'd drained the glass. 'I'll tell you tomorrow. *If* you win.'

Her eyes narrowed. 'Are you hustling me? You know, I can ask questions around town and find out everything I want to know.'

'Yes, but then you'd have to explain your sudden interest in my life,' he said, familiar with the workings of the town's gossip mill. 'As for myself, I'd rather get my answers straight from the horse's mouth, so to speak.'

'You've made your point.' She met his gaze without flinching. 'What's your question?'

He wanted to lose himself in her blue-gray eyes. Easy does it, he cautioned himself. 'Tell me about your summers here in Springwater.'

She sipped her water before she leaned back, running a finger around the edge of a worn spot on the forty-year-old table's gray Formica surface.

'My father was more mechanically minded than my uncle and grandfather, so he became an automotive repairman. I was three when there was an accident in the garage where he worked and he was killed. Since my mom didn't want me to grow up not knowing my dad's side of the family, she let me visit my uncle during the summers. The first time I stayed for several weeks I was Carrie's age.'

'It must have been frightening,' he said, thinking of Eunice's temperament.

'It was, but Uncle Earl took me under his wing. When I wasn't with him, I hung around my friend Mary Beth. I hardly ever saw Aunt Eunice except at mealtimes.'

'What did your mother do while you were gone?'

'My mom had become a teacher when I was little because her job as a store clerk didn't pay enough to support us. During the summers, she took classes to keep her certification current, so she was glad I had something to do while she studied. It really rankled Eunice because people spoke highly of my mom for becoming self-sufficient.'

That explained Eunice's scorn over Jenny giving her friend the same helping hand Earl had given her mother. Giving of oneself was obviously a legacy she'd learned from Earl.

'Every year, I spent six to eight weeks with my uncle until I graduated from high school. I loved those days.' She glanced around the sunny yellow kitchen. 'I can't believe he's gone. Everything looks just like it did back then. It amazes me how the refrigerator still works. They bought it in the early sixties.'

'I've wondered the same thing,' he said, eyeing the unit with its outdated lever-style handle.

'Sometimes I catch myself expecting to see him walk through the door and ask for a root beer float.'

Noah heard the catch in her voice and he reached over to touch her hand. 'I know what you mean,' he said. 'I visited here quite often myself.'

'I'd give up all this in a heartbeat,' she said, motioning with her free hand, 'to have him back. Some days, I'm so *angry* with him for leaving this to me.' She paused. 'You must think I'm a terrible person.'

'No,' he said. 'I think you're an honest one. Anger is one of the stages of grief, so what you're feeling is healthy. Where's your mom now?'

'She and a friend are motoring across America. I keep thinking she'll call and tell me I'm getting a stepfather, but it hasn't happened yet. Do you like to travel, too?'

'Hey,' he protested lightly, happy she'd freely shared more information about herself. 'You'll have to wait your turn to ask questions.'

She grinned. 'Then be prepared to lose.'

'Says who?' he said, pretending affront. In actuality, losing to Jenny wouldn't be a bad experience.

# CHAPTER SEVEN

THE next three weeks passed quickly. Jenny thought of the store now as hers rather than her uncle's. She'd arranged her stock to her liking and knew exactly what she had on hand and where to find it.

Noah arrived like clockwork every evening after he closed his office, and she found herself listening for his familiar footstep and throaty greeting. Although they'd played basketball often, the physical contact of their first game was never far from her mind. The more they were together, the more she longed to experience what she was certain would be a toe-curling kiss. Their chaperone, however, put a damper on the situation and so Jenny poured her frustrations into her work. Between the three of them, they refinished the antique pieces they'd dragged out of the basement and polished others to a high gloss, before turning them into display cases for her new shipments of goods.

After devoting exceptionally long hours to her projects during the past weekend, she came to work one Monday morning filled with an immeasurable sense of pride as she viewed the fruits of her labor.

A cherry-wood pie safe stood against one wall, filled with her new herbal products. A grouping of several round end tables and a newly restored trunk with polished brass fittings stood in the center of the room. Inside the trunk, a variety of sunscreen and sunburn products leaned against a collection of sand toys, children's sunglasses, a beach umbrella, and a floppy hat.

One table held a display of Medic-Alert bracelets and necklaces and the corresponding literature. On another, Carrie had stacked a variety of summer allergy products around a pot of silk flowers. Where she'd found the large plastic bumble-bee, Jenny didn't know, but it added a crowning touch to the display.

Now that her vision of modernizing the pharmacy had become a reality, Jenny decided to move into the next phase of her plan—providing services. She'd scheduled a PharmCo technician for fingerstick cholesterol screening as part of a promotion on cholesterol-lowering drugs. As soon as her funds permitted, she would install a blood-pressure machine for her customers. She'd also volunteered to work with the local health department during their diabetes screening clinics.

Things were definitely shaping up.

She retrieved the morning mail from the box outside the front entrance and began shuffling through the envelopes. Her heart skipped a beat as she came across two on distinctive personal stationery. Neither name nor return address were familiar.

Immediately she slit those open first. Inside both were letters of introduction and résumés—one from a pharmacist who'd heard about her job from a friend, the other from a woman who'd responded to her 'Help Wanted' ads.

Excitement bubbled inside as she scanned the letters again, hardly able to believe her good fortune. At long last, she'd finally generated interest in her job. Noah would be pleased to know that the fate of the pharmacy wouldn't hinge on a lack of personnel. If two people saw the possibilities of practicing in Springwater, then others might also.

To her surprise, her euphoric feeling soon passed, leaving in its wake one tinged with regret. She wouldn't be around to personally oversee the programs and services she'd worked so hard to implement.

On the heels of her startling discovery came the gentle reminder of her teaching contract. For the first time, she toyed with the idea of resigning her position at the high school, but her sense of preservation overruled it. She'd simply have to hire a manager who embraced her vision and would oversee her plans with the same enthusiasm.

Her resolve somewhat strengthened, she studied the candidates' curricula vitae and called each of them to schedule interviews.

Later, as she lay in bed, listening to Carrie's breathing across the hall, the creaks of the old house and the hoot of an owl, she discovered regret for something else as well.

Leaving meant an end to her evening workouts with Noah. Sure, she could find someone else to pit herself against, but her enjoyment had little to do with the actual exercise and everything to do with his company.

She'd learned that he loved history and liked to visit historical sites. He hadn't played basketball in college, but had been his high school's star forward for three years. His father had been a banker, his mother a secretary. They had divorced when he was thirteen.

Intuitively, she'd sensed a deep hurt in him as he'd recited the bare bones of the story. Perhaps, in time, he'd be more forthright.

She also admitted to counting the hours from the time he left until their next competition. Their question-and-answer period had been more rewarding than painful. The topics had been innocuous so far and she hesitated to ask something more personal, although she knew the moment was coming. Once she crossed the line separating general interest and deep soul-searching, he would reciprocate. She might be ready to see if his kiss came close to her fantasy, but she wasn't really sure she was ready for that.

Early the next morning, Mary Beth's daughter, Miranda, called and asked Carrie to spend the day at her house. Since it was Tuesday and time for summer kids' movies, Jenny couldn't say no. Her young charge deserved a break for working like a trouper. She'd stocked the shelves and tidied up the place to the point where even the dust motes fled in terror. The accumulation of odds and ends in the basement had waited this long for attention—they could wait a few more days.

Promptly at eleven o'clock, Jenny unlocked the front door. To her surprise, Herb was her first customer. The look on his face as he did a double-take on the room thrilled her to pieces.

'You really have changed things.' His gaze landed on her herbal product display. 'Was that the pie safe from the basement? It looks completely different.'

'It cleaned up nicely,' she said, remembering its condition only a few days ago. It had been stuffed with dog-eared ledgers, which they hadn't taken time to read, and the doors had hung loosely on broken hinges. 'I'm still amazed at what we found underneath all the old wax. It turned out to be a real treasure.'

His voice sounded flat. 'Yeah. A treasure.'

She got to business. 'What can I do for you?'

'I came by to see if you've run across some papers of mine. I'd run out of room at home, so Earl let me store a few boxes in the basement.'

'I'm afraid I've contributed to the mess down there,' she told him. 'If you want to look for them yourself, good luck.'

'Thanks,' he said. Twenty minutes later, he returned. 'They weren't where I thought they'd be.'

'We've been moving things around to get to the furniture, so I'm not surprised. When we start cleaning, I'll keep my eyes open.'

'I hate to make you go to the trouble on my account. I'll drop in again soon to dig around for myself. The papers aren't that important, but I'd hate to lose them. You know how the IRS can be when it comes to documentation for taxes.'

'I will,' she promised. In the next breath, she gave in to her impulsive question. 'By the way, I wanted to ask you about my uncle's bookkeeping.'

His black eyes grew wary. 'Yeah? What about it?'

'I noticed some discrepancies between the invoiced drugs and our inventory. We seem to be missing a great deal of stock.'

He visibly bristled. 'I don't recall anything missing before. If you're trying to pin something on me—'

'I'm not accusing you of anything,' she said, taken aback by his sudden hostility. 'The errors seemed too big to be clerical errors. I just thought you might have an explanation.'

He lifted his chin. 'I don't. Earl handled all the paperwork.'

She pressed on, hoping he'd drop a clue. 'Could he have loaned his stock to another pharmacy?'

He frowned. 'Why would he do that?'

'I don't know. It was just a thought.'

'Come to think of it, I do recall him saying something about it once. But he took care of the details, so I can't help you,' he reiterated, edging toward the door. 'If anything, you found some oversights. Your uncle didn't always function on all cylinders.'

She didn't like his innuendo. 'What are you saying?'

'Earl sometimes hit the hard stuff. He said it relaxed him. Take it from me, he came to work some days awfully relaxed.'

She stared at him, speechless for the few moments it took to understand his meaning. 'I don't believe my uncle was an alcoholic.'

He shrugged. 'Suit yourself.'

'Why haven't I heard this before now?'

'I covered for him. Not many people knew he hit the sauce. I was probably the only one. So if there are mistakes in the books, they were probably made on the days when Earl wasn't himself.'

'When did this start?' she asked, unable to grasp the idea of her uncle inebriated. If he hadn't touched a drop of liquor during the years of his stressful and loveless marriage, she couldn't imagine what had recently driven him to drink. 'Why?'

Once again, Herb shrugged. 'I wasn't his psychiatrist.' He glanced at his watch. 'I'd stay and visit, but I'm due at work.'

Her mind raced to sort through the new information. 'Sure. Thanks for stopping by.'

'You'll let me know if you find those boxes before I can look for them myself?' he asked.

'Yes.'

As soon as he'd left, Jenny went to her desk. Herb's accusation couldn't be true, but curiosity forced her to examine the ledgers.

Sure enough, the handwriting on certain days was more scrawled than on others. She'd thought it had meant her uncle's arthritis had flared up but, armed with Herb's news, she feared otherwise.

An unwelcome realization hit her and a new load of

guilt landed on her shoulders. Had alcohol been a factor in his fatal accident? Had he not been able to deal with his financial problems?

By leaving him alone for so long, pushing him out of her life, had she inadvertently been responsible for his death?

To Jenny's relief, she didn't have to preserve a brave front for Carrie's sake, but she still had to maintain some semblance of normalcy to her customers. It took every ounce of will-power in her body to make it through her day.

Too upset to eat during her lunch-break, she reached for the phone to call Noah. However, before she dialed the number, she realized what she was doing. She was about to pour out her troubles to him, which mean that at some point in the past few weeks she'd crossed the line defining their relationship. He wasn't a casual acquaintance any more. He'd suddenly become important—someone she could confide in, someone who would listen and be supportive, someone whose opinion she valued. When had she stepped over the boundaries she'd originally set for him?

And what did that mean? Was she falling in love with Noah?

She replaced the receiver as her mind staggered under the impact of her new-found knowledge. She didn't know what troubled her more—the mystery surrounding her uncle or her new attitude toward Noah. Although both issues presented unexpected complications, the situation with Noah would have longer-lasting consequences. If she grew to depend on him—to love him—it would be so hard to walk away. Almost impossible...

The doorbell broke her concentration and she reluctantly postponed her soul-searching to greet her customer.

With any luck, she'd have her thoughts and feelings in order before she saw Noah this evening.

'I'm a diabetic,' the forty-five-year-old man announced as she gave him her attention. He wore faded blue jeans, a blue T-shirt and a Chicago Cubs baseball cap. 'My glucose meter is on its last legs and I need a new one.'

'What brand do you have now?' she asked.

He gave her the particulars. 'I've had it a long time. In fact, I bought it when I was first diagnosed. That's been...' he scratched his head '...ten, twelve years, I'd say.'

'That model isn't made any more. There are several much more accurate ones on the market now. Take this one, for instance.' She pulled a unit off the shelf and placed it on the nearest counter. 'It uses less blood, is quicker, and holds its calibration longer. Also, the strips cost less than other brands so it's cheaper to operate in the long run.'

His eyes brightened. 'No kidding?'

'Yes. Here's how it works.' She took time to demonstrate its features, explain its memory capabilities, and discuss the storage of the strips and calibrator solutions.

'If you have any problems with it,' she said at the conclusion of her sales pitch, 'bring it back and I'll see if I can sort things out for you.'

'Sold!' he said, whipping out his check-book to sign his name—Rodney Meder—with a steady hand.

A long-haired, buxom peroxide blonde in her early twenties passed him on his way out. Rodney's eyes nearly bugged out of his head as he slowed his pace to plainly enjoy the view she presented.

Her black leather skirt barely covered her buttocks and her scoop-necked black vest-top clung to her chest as if she'd been poured into it. A rose tattoo was visible on her collar-bone and several other roses graced her arms and ankles. A pair of strappy high heels revealed red-painted toenails, and a silver bracelet circled one ankle. She'd covered her face liberally with make-up and two small silver hoops pierced her left eyebrow.

Jenny could only guess at what other body parts had been pierced as well, and she cringed at the thought of enduring the process.

The phone rang and she excused herself to answer it.

'How's it going today?' Noah asked in her ear.

Conscious of her customer waiting for service, Jenny didn't go into detail. 'I've had my moments.'

'Busy?'

'Right now, I am.' It wasn't the time to mention Herb's revelation.

'Then I'll keep this short,' he said, his tone becoming businesslike. 'Harriet Winkler just left my office. Two weeks ago, I started her on allopurinol. I want her to continue with the same daily 300-mg tablet.'

'For how long?'

'Thirty days. I may decrease it in two weeks, but if I do she can cut the pills in half. We'll see how her labs look. She'll be in shortly to pick it up.'

'I'll have it ready.'

'Are we still on for this evening?'

'Absolutely.' She didn't mean to sound frantic or worried, but she obviously did because his voice became concerned. She imagined a worry wrinkle on his forehead.

'Is everything OK?' he asked.

Jenny eyed the woman who was lingering by the herbal remedies. 'Yes. No. Maybe. Not really.' She sighed. 'I'll tell you about it tonight.'

She replaced the receiver, drew a deep breath and pasted a smile on her face. 'Hello.'

'Hi!' The girl popped the gum in her mouth. 'I need a prescription filled.'

Jenny accepted the slip of paper and deciphered the handwriting as a request for an anti-protozoal medication. Immediately, she guessed the woman had a *Trichomonas vaginalis* infection.

'It will be just a few minutes,' she advised her. 'You can either wait or come back.'

The girl popped her gum again. 'I'll wait.'

Jenny checked the name recorded. 'I'm sorry, but I can't read your last name.'

'It's Budd. My name's Rose Budd.' Rose smiled as she popped her gum. 'It's my stage name. Kinda cute, isn't it?'

'Very unusual,' Jenny agreed, understanding the significance of the rose tattoos over her body. 'You're not from around here, are you?'

'I'm only in town for a few days. I'm dancing over at The Ruby Slipper this week. If you're free, drop in tonight and bring your friends.'

'Thanks for the invitation,' Jenny said with a straight face as she carefully counted out the prescribed amount of tablets. She'd seen the ads in the paper featuring this week's draw-card of strippers. 'Unfortunately, I have other plans.'

'Too bad. Maybe you can make it Friday. The club will have something special for everyone.' Rose winked.

Jenny doubted if Rose's idea of 'something special' matched hers. The fellows who managed to book a private showing with Rose would take home more than just a pleasant memory. They'd have the dubious honor of paying twice for their evening—once to Rose and once to their doctor. It would be interesting to see how many

Springwater men would drop by in the weeks ahead to fill similar prescriptions.

'Here you go,' she told the dancer. 'Take one tablet three times a day for seven days.'

'Seven days! Are you sure that's right? My friend's been on this and she took it all in one day.'

'She may have,' Jenny said. Since the dosage regimen was individualized, sometimes the physician requested a one-day treatment if compliance was an issue. In Rose's case, Jenny could easily imagine the woman forgetting her pills on a regular basis. She could also imagine how fast Rose could spread the disease to unsuspecting men and their wives if her infection went uncontrolled.

'I can only give you what the doctor has ordered. If you'd like it changed, you'll have to call him.'

Rose popped her gum. 'Nah. It's OK. Seven days. Gotcha.'

'Three times a day,' she reminded her.

'Three a day. I'll remember.'

Jenny hoped so. 'You should also avoid alcohol for the next eight days.'

'Oh, I always do. I only drink beer.'

If Rose was trying to be an example of a 'dumb blonde', she had succeeded. 'I meant anything alcoholic. No beer.'

'My friend says it doesn't bother her.'

'The drug reacts with alcohol and can cause abdominal cramps, nausea, vomiting and headaches,' Jenny patiently explained. It created a reaction similar to what Antabuse gave alcoholics, but she knew the information would go over Ms Budd's head. 'If your friend hasn't experienced it, she's lucky. Most people do. It's best not to take the chance unless you don't mind being violently ill.'

Once again, Rose shrugged as if the subject was of little importance. 'OK. No beer.'

She dug in her voluminous bag and withdrew a thick billfold. As Jenny quoted the price, Rose opened up one fold, revealing a thick wad of greenbacks, and pulled out the correct denomination.

Ever polite, Jenny rang up the sale and said, 'Thanks for stopping by.'

'If you change your mind about Friday, let me know. I'll guarantee you the best seat in the house.'

'I'll keep it in mind.'

Rose left and Jenny succumbed to an urge to wash her hands. Rose, her medical condition notwithstanding, was clean and neat, but Jenny had seen the microscopic trichomonads during their hospital's Lab Week Open House one year. After watching the protozoa swim around the slide, propelled by their flagella and appearing only slightly larger than a white blood cell, just thinking of the little critters brought on a desire to wash her hands.

Her reaction was somewhat ridiculous since they were spread through sexual contact but, nevertheless, she couldn't help herself.

Just as she left the tiny bathroom, the bell above the door tinkled and the sight of the woman entering brought a quiet groan to Jenny's throat. Twyla Beach had been a crony of her Aunt Eunice, which didn't say much for her. The two had fed off each other's complaints and what one hadn't thought of, the other had.

Before she could welcome her into the store, Twyla's sharp eyes scanned the room. Jenny imagined the cogs in her brain turning with cost calculations of her remodeling project. She didn't have to stretch her imagination to know that Twyla would report everything she saw.

She stiffened her spine. Twyla could draw her own conclusions because Eunice had received more than her fair share.

'I've come for a refill,' she said without preamble.

'Do you have the number?' Jenny asked politely.

'I haven't needed it before in all the years I've patronized this place.'

'It's just easier to look up the records if I have a number.'

'Well, I don't have it.'

'No problem. Have a seat.'

Jenny quickly filled her script for a diuretic. Twyla paid her bill and left in a huff, acknowledging Harriet Winkler on her way out with a mere nod.

'Old grouch,' Harriet mumbled as she approached. Her footsteps were sure and the cane seemed more window-dressing than a necessity.

'Good afternoon, Mrs Winkler,' Jenny said. 'How are you today?'

Harriet smiled. 'Fine. I wonder if Dr Kimball has called in a prescription for me?'

'Yes, he has. I'll have it ready in just a few minutes if you'd like to wait. If not, I can drop it by your house later this evening.'

Harriet crossed both hands to lean on her cane. 'Nonsense. I'm not in any hurry. Gina's covering the store right now. She reminds me of you at that age, you know.'

Jenny labelled a bottle with Harriet's information and the medication instructions. 'She does?'

'Oh, my, yes. She's so full of energy and so eager to please. It's such a shame that her father is such a ne'er-do-well. Still, I'm hoping she'll win a few scholarships and go to college. She wants to be a librarian.'

'How nice.' She counted out thirty pills and dumped

them in the bottle. 'Would you prefer a regular lid instead of a childproof cap?'

'Yes, please,' Harriet said briskly, before returning to her subject. 'Gina has one year of high school left, so I'm steering her toward the organizations who give money to worthy students. I'm sure she'd appreciate any leads you might have.'

'I don't know of any at the moment, but if I do I'll pass along the information.' Jenny slid the bottle into a small sack and handed it to her. 'All done. Take one a day, just like before.'

'I will. I've seen what a difference the medication makes. My father had gout, you know.'

'No, I didn't.'

'He, of course, suffered terribly. I'm sure they didn't have the drugs to ease the pain, like they do today.'

'Probably not.'

Harriet's eyes twinkled. 'Ah, he was a crusty old boy. He didn't cotton to people telling him what to do. He loved all the foods he shouldn't have. Liver, sardines, lentils. My mother quit buying his beer—he loved Coors—but he always managed to find one somewhere.'

The items Harriet had mentioned, including wine, anchovies and sweetbreads, were rich in purines. When metabolized, they broke down into uric acid. If the compound wasn't excreted through the kidneys, excessive amounts crystallized to form kidney stones or were deposited in joint spaces. Gout, or gouty arthritis, was the result. For this reason, doctors instructed their patients to avoid those particular foods.

'I'll bet he paid the price for his disobedience.'

Harriet's smile grew broad. 'Yes, he did. But after the current episode had passed, he'd tell me that indulging in his favorites now and again was worth the pain. For myself, I can't agree. Nothing—absolutely *nothing*—is worth that kind of suffering.'

She leaned closer and winked. 'Although I must admit, I have nipped my wine on special occasions. It's my way of living vicariously. Being an armchair traveller isn't always enough. Nor is observing all the goings-on in town.'

'I suppose not.'

'You wouldn't believe half of the things I could tell you, but they're all true. Each and every one.' The flowers on her hat bobbed as she nodded. 'I'm not bragging, mind you, but I've lived here a lot of years and I could write a book about the skeletons in people's closets.'

Harriet's knowledge could either be a blessing or a curse, but Jenny had to know the truth. 'Can I ask you something?'

Harriet tapped her cane on the floor and smiled benevolently. 'Of course, dear.'

The phone rang and Jenny was frustrated by the poor timing. 'Go ahead and answer. I'm not in any hurry.'

Twyla Beach was on the phone. 'You gave me the wrong pills.'

'No, I didn't,' Jenny patiently explained.

'These aren't the same size or shape as the ones I've taken before.'

'My supplier changed. I dispensed the same drug, but it's a generic form and much cheaper than the name brand. Your doctor OK'd the substitution.'

'Well,' the woman huffed across the line, 'I'd better not suffer any side effects, or you'll hear from me again.' Before Jenny could reply, she heard a loud click in her ear.

Another happy customer, she thought facetiously as she returned to Harriet's side. 'Now, where were we?'

'You were going to ask me a question,' Harriet prompted.

'Oh, yes. Did…' Jenny swallowed hard, summoning the courage to accept the older woman's answer, however unpleasant it might be. 'Did my uncle drink?'

'Why, of course he did.' At this Jenny's heart sank. 'Your uncle belonged to a wine club. They had tasting parties once a month.' Her gaze narrowed. 'I suspect, though, you're really asking if he drank to excess.'

Jenny cleared the lump in her throat. 'Yes.'

Harriet stared at her kindly. 'I never saw him do anything of the sort, child. That's not to say he didn't tie one on as men sometimes do, but I rather doubt it. He wasn't the type—too much in control. What makes you suspect he had a problem?'

'Something Herb said in passing.'

'Herb?' Harriet stiffened her spine, raised her chin and narrowed her gaze. 'Why, that little weasel! How dare he slander a good man, especially when Earl can't defend himself.'

'Herb did work with Uncle Earl on a daily basis,' Jenny reminded her.

Harriet stomped her cane. 'That may be, but I for one wouldn't believe it unless I saw physical evidence.'

Evidence. Jenny's spirits rose. If her uncle had drunk as Herb claimed, there would be bottles at home. Organizing the pharmacy had been her top priority—she hadn't bothered to sift through his personal possessions.

'The next time I see Herb I'm going to give him a piece of my mind,' Harriet railed. 'The nerve of that man! He should be drummed out of town.'

The retired teacher squared her shoulders, then patted Jenny's hand. 'Don't worry, child. I haven't heard this rumor before and I've lived here a lot of years. Herb was probably just being hateful to you. I hear he's a real pill if things don't go his way. Consider the source and ignore whatever he's told you.'

'I'll try.' Jenny drew some comfort from Harriet's vehement endorsement of her uncle's character. Regardless, she intended to search her house from top to bottom if for no other reason than to ease her mind.

The moment she pulled into her driveway after she closed the store, she slammed the car into 'Park,' checked on Bugs who was sleeping his afternoon away, then hurried inside. Without wasting a moment, she flung open each kitchen cabinet to peer at its contents. She found all sorts of beautiful dishes and glassware which she would have taken time to study under other circumstances.

After finishing her search in the kitchen, she moved to the formal dining room where she rummaged through the buffet and china cupboard. She was about to start elsewhere when she spied the narrow door to the small, slender cupboard built in one corner under the staircase.

It took several hard yanks to gain access. The interior was shadowed, but she could see the contents well enough thanks to the sunlight streaming through the south window.

Bottle after bottle of every size and shape imaginable stood in neat rows on the two shelves like soldiers in parade formation.

She touched the closest bottle—a fifth of Johnny Walker whisky. The glass was cool and hard, the contents half-gone.

The stiffening drained out of her knees and she sank onto the floor. Sitting in front of the opening, she drew her knees to her chest and curled her arms around them as she stared mindlessly at the offending evidence.

Working day and night for the past few weeks to restore

her heritage had eased her guilt for not joining the family business sooner. The idea of her uncle drowning his sorrows because she hadn't fulfilled her long-ago agreement to become his partner ate at her like acid on metal.

She'd paid for her past sins with her career. How could she pay for this one?

A brisk knock brought her out of her daze. Before she could summon the energy to rise, Noah's voice echoed through the house.

'Anybody home?' he called.

'In here,' she returned.

Noah strode into the kitchen and did a double-take at the sight awaiting him. Cabinet doors stood ajar, including several of those well out of normal reach. A chair was positioned near one counter, plainly used as a step stool.

A sense of foreboding came over him. 'Jenny?'

'I'm in the dining room.'

He found her on the floor, staring into the recesses of a cupboard. He didn't know what to think but, sensing an unhealthy tension in the atmosphere, he tried to ease it. 'It looks like a tornado went through the kitchen,' he said. 'Did you find what you were looking for?'

She didn't answer. He was about to repeat his question when she spoke. 'Yes, I did.'

'Which is?' he prompted, puzzled by her reaction.

The raw pain in her eyes stabbed at him. 'Was alcohol involved in my uncle's car accident?'

'Alcohol?' he echoed. 'Are you suggesting that Earl was drinking?'

'Yes.'

He shook his head, certain he hadn't heard correctly. 'What in heaven's name gave you that goofy idea?'

The breath she took sounded shaky. 'I asked Herb about

the missing inventory. According to him, my uncle drank to the point where he couldn't do his job.'

He was incredulous. 'And you believed him?'

'Not at first.'

Her search now made sense. 'Until you found his stash,' he said, motioning to the cupboard.

'It explains the shaky handwriting, the gaps in the bookkeeping, the financial drain.'

'It might,' he conceded. 'Except for one critical point of fact. Earl didn't drink.'

She jumped to her feet. 'How can you be sure?'

'Because I am. Earl enjoyed a glass of wine now and again. Do you?'

'Yes, but—'

'So do I. Does that make us alcoholics?'

Instead of answering, she pointed. 'What about the evidence?'

'So everyone in town who has liquor in his cabinet has a drinking problem?'

'As you can see, there are twelve bottles involved,' she said tartly. 'Not just one. How would you interpret the evidence?'

Noah rubbed his jaw as he studied the situation. As far as he was concerned, Herb had some explaining to do for trying to discredit Earl. However, he would deal with him later. For now, he had to convince Jenny of the truth.

Noah pulled the bottle of Johnny Walker off the shelf and placed it on the antique dining room table. 'Take a good look at this and tell me what you see.'

# CHAPTER EIGHT

JENNY glanced at it. 'The bottle's half-empty,' she said flatly.

'Yeah. What else?'

A wrinkle appeared between her eyebrows. 'I don't know. You tell me.'

Noah swiped the shoulders of the glass and held up his finger. 'What do you see?'

'Dust.' A glimmer of understanding began to shine in her eyes.

'Now look at the shelf.'

She crouched down for a closer look, then stared up at him, her eyes glimmering. 'There's a dust-free circle.'

'Exactly. If Earl drank consistently, there wouldn't be any dust. Also, this is a rotten location to store anything you're going to use on a daily basis. The door, as I recall, sticks and a person has to practically crawl on the floor to put anything inside. If he was a closet drinker, he'd store his poison in a more accessible place.

'I can also tell you,' he pressed on, 'that during the holidays he hosted a big Christmas party for his customers. All of this is probably left over from that evening.'

'Do you really think so?' She sounded as if she wanted to believe him, but was also afraid to take that final step.

He decided to nudge her along. 'As for his accident, drug-testing is commonly done on the drivers, especially if injuries result. Your uncle's test was clean. So was the trucker's.'

Tears glistened in her eyes and the tension holding her

spine seemed to disappear. Unable to help himself, he
touched her back and opened his arms. Without further
encouragement, she entered his embrace.

'Thank you,' she whispered. 'I really should have
known better. He gave up smoking because of its harmful
effects. It didn't make sense for him to substitute alcohol
for nicotine.'

Her lips brushed against his cheek as she clearly meant
to show her appreciation for the peace of mind he'd given
her. That simple act, however, ruined his. His control tee-
tered precariously on the edge of a slippery slope.

He drew a bracing breath and forced his thoughts back
to the conversation. 'No, it didn't.'

She tilted her head to meet his gaze. 'Why do you suppose…?' Her voice died as if she had suddenly become
aware of her position. Suddenly aware of how her curves
and his angles fit together like puzzle pieces. Suddenly
aware of the husky quality in his voice.

Every nerve went on alert as he waited for an imper-
ceptible signal as to what he should—or could—do next.
If he'd felt the slightest nudge, the smallest indication that
she wanted to escape, he would have released her, albeit
reluctantly.

She'd clearly read the question in his mind as her gaze
travelled to his mouth and back again. Her eyes shone
with something—permission, perhaps?—that whittled
away at his restraint. Her breath whispered through
slightly parted lips that seemed to beg for contact with
his.

Noah didn't need a second invitation. He'd intended to
go slowly, but as soon as he made contact nothing could
have separated them. Her sweet taste fueled a hunger of
monumental and almost frightening proportions.

Her arms slid upwards to circle his neck. Her hands ran

through the hair on the back of his head and she raised herself on tiptoe to settle herself more comfortably against his chest.

He ran his hands along each side of her torso, his thumbs grazing the underside of her lush breasts. Flames seemed to surround him, flames that longed to be quenched in one particular manner, even though he knew it was too soon in their tenuous relationship to expect such a gift.

Patricia may have broken her promise and left him standing at the altar, but at this very moment he wanted to thank her. In fact, he couldn't remember what she looked like because Jenny had filled his thoughts so completely. He'd thought he'd never get over the humiliation he'd suffered, but having Jenny in his arms soothed his wounded ego like a healing balm.

Regardless, if he didn't call a halt to this, he'd reach the point of no return. Reluctantly, he cooled his jets and shifted position. Jenny's dazed and bewildered expression was worth more to him than if he'd been offered a new addition to Springwater's fifteen-bed hospital with all the latest equipment money could buy.

Jenny stared at Noah, surprised at how quickly passion had flared between them. She'd intended her kiss to be platonic, a sign of appreciation. Instead, she'd been swept away in a flash flood of desire.

Aware of her arms still entwined around his neck, of her fingers toying with his hair, she stilled her hands. Part of her wanted to jump out of his embrace and pretend this had never happened. The other part wanted to revel in the experience and prolong it for another eight hours. She'd kissed a fair number of men in her lifetime, but those encounters seemed like the moves of a fumbling adolescent in comparison.

The questions plaguing her earlier in the day now seemed answered. Their relationship *had* proceeded to a new level, although she was still hesitant to categorize her feelings as 'love.' Regardless, her actions would set the tone for the future and, oh, how she wanted to consider a future!

She chose to acknowledge the magnetism between them rather than ignore it.

Stroking the back of his neck, she asked, 'So tell me how a man who packs such a powerful kiss is still unmarried?'

A lazy grin tugged at the corners of his mouth and his eyes sparkled behind his lenses. 'No fair, asking questions.'

'Why not?'

'I haven't lost tonight's game.'

She was incredulous. Her knees were too shaky and she certainly wasn't in the right frame of mind to do justice to her sport. 'Do you still want to play?'

'I'm willing to call a tie if you are.'

'OK.'

One eyebrow lifted and he tightened his hold as if he'd expected her to run, both physically and emotionally. 'And we both ask questions?'

Jenny nodded, aware that her decision had lifted the unspoken limits each had imposed. Tonight's discussion would explore deeply personal topics—sensitive subjects that she didn't want to touch with the proverbial ten-foot pole. Yet maybe it was time to clear the air.

'For the record,' he began quietly, 'the bride left him at the altar.'

Stunned, she let her hands drop to his biceps as she took a step back, pleased at how he allowed her the distance but didn't relinquish contact. 'She left you?'

He shrugged. 'Yeah. The entire wedding party came down the aisle as the pianist played the entrance song. Instead of Patricia's father escorting her in, he came alone.'

'How awful.'

'It wasn't one of the happier days in my life,' he admitted.

'I don't imagine it was,' she said, aware of an ache building in her heart for the shame, disappointment, and rejection he must have felt.

'I should have seen it coming,' he said. 'She reminded me of a butterfly, flitting from one thing to another. No matter what it was, school, a job, her apartment, she wasn't satisfied with it for long. I should have expected to fall in the same category.'

How shallow, Jenny thought in righteous indignation. She'd love to scold this woman for the prize she'd let slip through her fingers.

'It was a long time ago,' he said. 'And best forgotten.'

'Yes, it is,' she agreed, although she wondered if he'd truly forgotten or was simply trying to convince himself. From the way he'd reacted so strongly when she'd originally announced her plans to go out of business, she suspected that the wound of rejection hadn't fully healed. To Noah, promises were like rules—they weren't made to be broken, even if there were times when a broken promise worked out for the best.

Even if the broken promise saved him from an unsuitable marriage.

'Better luck next time.'

'Maybe,' he said, his tone noncommittal. 'But I doubt there will be a next time.'

'Why do you say that?'

'If I choose to marry, we're going to elope.'

'What if she wants the works? It's her ceremony, too.'

He shrugged. 'I'm not planning on getting married, so it's a moot point.'

It didn't make sense, but his entire attitude saddened her. His name evoked biblical images of pairs which his near-constant presence had enhanced over the past few weeks. Apparently her sense of being one-half of a couple was horribly one-sided. The hope of excitement rising within her seemed to wither under his declaration. Her expectations had obviously leapt further ahead than his had. Perhaps she would be wise to approach this in the same, slow manner that he did. After all, she *was* leaving Springwater. It would be best if neither of them got their emotions tangled up before then. Unfortunately, she was afraid that her decision had come too late.

He glanced around. 'Where's Carrie?'

'Is that your question for the evening?' she asked innocently, following his lead to drop the subject although she wanted to discuss this further.

He pulled her close until they were nose to nose. 'Not on your life,' he said, his growl plainly all show and no substance.

Jenny didn't think she'd slip past his turn so easily, but it had been worth a try. 'She's at Miranda's house. She'll be home some time this evening.'

'Do we have time to go out to eat?' he asked.

'Not really. She's supposed to be home by seven and it's already six-fifteen. How about a BLT?'

'Bacon-lettuce-tomato. My favorite,' he said. 'What can I do to help?'

Letting him go was bittersweet. Jenny would have liked to have remained nestled against him for several more hours, but the prospect of later comforted her.

She put him to work, slicing the tomatoes, washing the

lettuce and toasting the bread while she microwaved the bacon and prepared a pitcher of peach-flavored iced tea.

Later, while they were eating, she posed the question she'd tried to ask before his kiss had sidetracked her. 'Why did Herb say those things if they weren't true? What would he gain?'

'It's hard to say. It sounds more like sour grapes on his part.'

'I'm sorry Uncle Earl didn't leave a portion of his business to him but, taking his frustrations out on me, it won't change a thing.'

'No,' Noah said, 'But you're here and Earl isn't.'

'So I'm the scapegoat.'

'Exactly. He knows better than to spread gossip about Earl now. Herb may be working in Hays, but he still lives in Springwater. People won't tolerate anyone who tarnishes Earl's memory.'

Jenny certainly hoped so. She bore responsibility for a lot of things in her life, and she'd hate to add ruining her uncle's reputation to the list.

Her choice of the word 'ruin' sparked a new worry. After their high-voltage kiss, Noah wouldn't look favorably on her news of two possible replacements. And that certainly wasn't the sort of news she could keep from him. If nothing else, she owed him honesty.

'By the way,' she said, plunging into her task before she lost her courage, 'two applications came in yesterday's mail. Both people have great credentials, so I've asked them to come for interviews.'

Momentary surprise flared in his eyes. 'Then you've given up the idea of completely selling out?'

'I suppose I have,' she said, somewhat amazed by the turn of events. Selling had been at the top of her list of options, while finding a pharmacist had come in a distant second. Somewhere along the line, probably after she'd incorporated her family's antiques into the decor and stamped her own personality on the place, her priorities had shifted.

'Why not just stay here yourself?'

'I can't,' she said, willing him to understand her position. 'I have a teaching contract. Even if I wanted to break it, I couldn't, without paying a huge penalty. I've sunk every spare dollar into the pharmacy, so I can't afford to do that.'

She had slowly regained her confidence in her abilities, but it was easy to be confident, knowing that teaching acted as her escape hatch. And if the truth were known, she wasn't convinced that she could handle pharmacy work on a long-term basis.

He leaned forward and planted his elbows on the table. 'What if your two applicants don't work out?'

She hadn't let herself dwell on the possibility because she didn't have a solution figured out for that scenario. 'I'm keeping my fingers crossed that at least one of them *is* suitable. I don't have a lot of time to hold out for someone else. It's already the end of June, which means I only have about six weeks before I start back for school.'

'I see.' When he spoke, his tone was deceptively calm. 'Shall I ask my question before or after we do the dishes?'

Her smile froze on her face. She sensed the topic was one she'd rather not have discussed but, as much as wanted to, she couldn't change the rules now.

She thought about waiting until they'd washed the dishes and stacked them in the cupboards, but she didn't want to prolong the inevitable.

Her stomach knotted. 'Before,' she replied, striving to present a calm and unruffled demeanor.

She felt like a specimen under the microscope as he studied her through his glasses.

'Why did you give up everything to become a teacher?'

Before Jenny could decide where to begin her story, the kitchen door opened and Carrie breezed in, along with a wave of heat.

'I'm home,' she called, all smiles. 'Miss me?'

Jenny felt like a pardoned prisoner. 'I certainly did. How was your day?'

'Great! Absolutely, positively wonderful. Can I do it again?'

Jenny was pleased by Carrie's enthusiasm. At least one of them had enjoyed a carefree eight hours. 'Sure. Why not?'

'Tomorrow?' the girl asked.

'Not tomorrow. Maybe toward the end of the week.'

Noah interrupted. 'Looks like you soaked up some sun, kiddo.'

'We did,' Carrie said proudly. 'We stayed at the pool all afternoon.'

'Your skin looks awfully red,' Jenny said. 'Did you wear sunblock?'

'Oh, yes. Miranda's mom made us.' Carrie sniffed the air. 'I smell bacon.'

'We had BLTs. Do you want one?'

'Nah. We already ate. Boy, Miranda has the neatest bedroom. She's got stars and planets painted on her walls and ceiling. They glow in the dark. Maybe my mom will let me do that, too.'

Jenny doubted if the decision rested with Susan. The landlord had a lot to say about what the tenants could and couldn't do and 'no' ranked high on his list of favored responses. Since it was easier to have every unit the same in terms of upkeep, his decorating tastes ran along strict generic lines. She didn't envy Susan the task of breaking the news to her daughter that glow-in-the-dark permanent decorations were forbidden.

For the next thirty minutes, Carrie chattered non-stop. Jenny exchanged glances with Noah, aware of how patiently he was waiting for the child to wind down from her fun-filled day.

Just as Jenny was about to send Carrie upstairs to get ready for bed, Noah's beeper sounded. He read the message display, then borrowed her phone to call the ER. When he returned, he had disappointment written all over his rugged features.

'I've got to go,' he said.

'Anything serious?'

'Seizures in a child.'

She mentally ran through her list of patrons. 'It's not Mary Beth's son, Luke?'

'No.'

Although she was glad Mary Beth wasn't suffering agony right now, she felt sympathy for the unknown parents. 'I usually don't go to bed until eleven. If you want to stop by later, I'll be awake.'

He stroked the side of her face with an index finger. 'I want to, very much.'

'I'll leave the light on,' she promised.

Noah's departure made the house seem lonely, which was ridiculous since Carrie talked continuously about her exciting day.

For the next few hours Jenny rehearsed her speech, and jumped at the sound of each car driving by. At one point a car door slammed and she peered through the curtains, looking for Noah's familiar Blazer. However, it had been the neighbors coming home.

Perhaps he'd decided to maintain his distance now that

she'd announced her intent to leave Springwater in six weeks. Maybe the child's case had been more complicated than expected. That had to be it, she decided. Noah wasn't the type to give up before he got answers to his questions.

Time dragged as she tried to second-guess the reasons for his absence. Finally, at eleven-thirty, she ended her lonely vigil. Tomorrow would arrive far too soon in some respects, and too slowly in others.

The next afternoon, Gloria Patterson, a widow in her early seventies, stood in front of the display of vitamins and minerals, her forehead puckered as she studied each bottle.

Frustrated by columns of figures which never added up to the same amount, Jenny gratefully abandoned her ledgers in favor of her customer. 'May I help you?' she asked.

'I certainly hope so,' Mrs Patterson said tartly. 'Dr Ingram wants me to take Vitamin B12, but I don't see it on the shelf.'

'B12 is a prescription drug and is given as an injection.'

'Injection?' Her eyes narrowed. 'Are you sure? He didn't say anything about that.'

'Did he give you a prescription?' Jenny asked.

Her hands crippled with arthritis, Mrs Patterson pulled a scrap of paper out of her purse. 'No. He just wrote the name down and said I needed this.'

The words 'Vitamin B12' were scrawled on a plain piece of paper, like one might use for a grocery list.

'I wanted to show it to my daughter. She's a nurse, you know. Checks out everything I take. Can't be too careful these days. Doctors want to give you a pill for everything, even if you don't need it.'

'That's nice you have someone who can explain the medications to you,' Jenny said. More likely, Mrs Patterson's daughter had to persuade the woman to take her pills. 'But that vitamin isn't available over the counter like the others. Did Dr Ingram say you had to come back again?'

'Next month.'

'Did he mention anything about getting a shot?' Jenny asked.

'Oh, I got one today. I just thought I'd stop in and see if I could buy this for myself. Doctors charge so much for things these days.'

'Unfortunately, that particular vitamin can't be purchased as an oral medication.'

Gloria lifted a vial of B6. 'Now why can't I just take two of these? Two B6s should add up to one B12.'

Jenny smiled. 'I'm afraid it doesn't work that way. They are two different vitamins because their chemical make-up is different.' She wondered if she should tell her the scientific names of pyridoxine and cobalamin, then decided against it. Mrs Patterson wasn't interested in a biochemistry lecture.

Gloria sniffed, as if she didn't believe Jenny's explanation. Jenny hoped her daughter—the nurse—could get through to her since she herself could not.

'If you ask me, it's a racket. Pure and simple.'

'Maybe Dr Ingram will write an order so you can purchase the vial and your daughter can give you the injection.'

Gloria's gaze sharpened. 'Really?'

'Of course. It's done all the time.'

'Then I'm going back over there right now,' she declared. 'I see the doctor often enough as it is, without going for something like this, too. I'll be back, or my name isn't Gloria Patterson.'

Jenny watched the lady leave. As determined as Gloria

was, she wouldn't rest until she'd arranged the situation to suit herself.

For the next hour, she helped one man—a golfer—find an allergy product for his hay fever, cautioned a woman to drink lots of fluids while she took a sulfa derivative for a urinary tract infection, and assisted an elderly lady with finding the right heating pad.

Just as she rang up the last sale, a young man in his early twenties, wearing dusty overalls and sporting grease under his fingernails, walked in and headed for the opposite end of the store.

Jenny handed the package to Mrs Stafford and watched the fellow out of the corner of one eye. 'Thanks for coming by.'

As soon as the lady left, Jenny went over to offer her assistance. 'May I help you find something.'

He rose from his search of the lower shelves, his face as red as a cherry tomato. 'I'm looking for a box of...' He mumbled his last word.

'Pardon me?' she asked, trying to figure out what he was looking for.

'Condoms. I want a box of condoms.'

Obviously he wasn't accustomed to making such a purchase. 'Right around the corner,' she said in her most professional voice, as if they were discussing the location of aspirin. The naughty thought of him paying Ms Rose Budd a visit came to mind, but she quickly pushed it aside. What he did on his own time was his own business.

Taking pity on him for being so ill at ease, she slid the box of twelve into a brown paper bag, before taking his money and sending him on his way.

Noah called a few minutes later to prescribe an antibiotic for one of his young patients. 'Do you have any earplugs to fit a five-year-old?'

'Yes, I believe I do.'

'Good,' he said. 'According to her mother, Ariel gets swimmer's ear every year, so I've recommended buying a set.'

'I'll have them ready in case she asks for them,' Jenny promised.

His tone became less businesslike. 'I'm sorry I couldn't make it back last night. I ended up seeing three of my patients instead of one.'

'I understand,' she said. Doctors' hours weren't always nine to five, even in a small town. 'How's the seizure patient?'

'He's OK. His valproic acid dosage isn't adequate now that he's gone through a recent growth spurt, but we'll see what the neurologist says. By the way, what's Carrie doing today? Slaving away to make up for her day off yesterday?'

She laughed. 'Actually, she's at home. Her sunburn's pretty painful and she's rather miserable right now. Apparently her sunblock didn't have a high enough SPF or wasn't as waterproof as the label claimed.'

'So you probably can't make a movie tonight?'

Jenny would have loved to have said yes. She not only wanted to see Tom Hanks and Meg Ryan in their romantic comedy, but she'd also enjoy spending the evening with Noah. 'I'd better stay home,' she said, her voice filled with regret. 'Carrie's going to need some TLC.'

'I'll bring ice cream after dinner to cheer her up,' he offered.

'Good idea. She'll like that.'

'And how does her temporary guardian feel about it?'

Hearing the lilt in his voice, she imagined his smile. 'Oh, she's looking forward to it,' she said, referring to his presence rather than the actual treat.

'Rocky Road or strawberry cheesecake?'

'Vanilla,' she corrected. 'We'll have root beer floats. She's been begging for them and I haven't indulged her yet. Since she's going home right after the July Fourth holiday, I can't postpone it much longer.'

'Vanilla, it is. By the way, I saw your flyers for next week's cholesterol screening. You should get a decent turnout.'

'I hope so,' she said fervently. 'I want people to come in and see that Ruscoe Pharmacy is more than just a place to go when they're sick. In fact, I'm crossing my fingers that people will notice my new line of herbal supplements.'

She thought of the ledgers lying on her desk. While she couldn't predict long-term results as yet, she did see some promise in her finances.

'They'd better notice those. After moving your pie safe to be part of the display, I needed a chiropractor.'

She grinned at his aggrieved, but obviously faked tone. 'Poor thing. If you're wanting me to pay for a session with Harriet's relative, you're out of luck.'

'I had a different therapist in mind.'

The suggestion in his voice brought a warm glow to her insides. 'You're either not busy this afternoon, or you're not where anyone can hear you.'

'Right, both times.'

The bell rang over the door and Jenny watched a mother and young child walk in. 'I can't say the same. Gotta go. I think the earplug mom is here.'

'See you this evening.' Noah cradled the receiver, leaned back in his chair and steepled his fingers. He was eager to see Jenny again, even though they'd parted company not too many hours ago. She was like a fine wine and he savored every taste. And, like a true connoisseur, the anticipation added to the enjoyment.

Della poked her head through his half-open doorway. 'Harriet is here to see you.'

'Is she ill?'

'She says she's not, but she insists on talking to you.'

He rose. 'Then send her in.'

Della motioned for Harriet to enter his office while he quickly unloaded a pile of medical journals off his extra chair. 'Have a seat,' he offered.

Harriet shook her head so vehemently that the flowers on her hat bent in half. 'I can't. I'm too wrought up.'

He perched on the edge of his desk. 'What's wrong?'

'It's terrible. I think the man should be tarred and feathered.'

'What's terrible? Who should be tarred and feathered?'

'Herb Kravitz, that's who,' Harriet declared. 'Do you know what that man has done?'

A sense of foreboding came over him. 'No.'

'He's spreading rumors all over town about our Jenny.' She waved her arms wildly. 'He's saying that she's incompetent.'

'How ridiculous.'

'Yeah, well, that's not all. He's also saying that she was forced to quit her pharmacy job.' She paused. 'Because she killed someone.'

## CHAPTER NINE

Noah listened, stunned by Harriet's revelation and yet not wholly surprised. Jenny had been very secretive about her reasons for turning her back on her medical career. The story circulating around town could explain her initial reluctance to personally take over the Ruscoe Pharmacy day-to-day operations.

However, if he remembered their conversation correctly, she hadn't said that she *couldn't* take over. She'd only said that she *wouldn't*. He might be splitting hairs, but there was a difference between the two.

'He's stirring the whole town into a frenzy,' Harriet said, her tone sharp. 'After he told Jenny that ridiculous story about Earl, I warned him to mind his p's and q's because I wouldn't stand for it and neither would anybody else. Now he's started in on poor Jenny.'

'When did you hear this?'

'Two people came into my store today, upset over what Herb had said, and rightly so. I tried to tell them the story was unfounded, but I'm not sure I convinced them. After a third person carried the same rumor to me, I knew I had to talk to you.'

'Where did he get his information?'

Harriet threw her hands up in the air. 'Who knows? Somehow, he's hooked up with Twyla Beach and she's spreading it, too. Of course, she's adding her personal experience as supporting evidence. Says Jenny gave her different pills than what she's taken for years. This whole affair is horribly disconcerting.'

'You don't believe Herb, do you?' Harriet's endorsement of causes usually guaranteed victory, so if Harriet stood on Jenny's side she had a good chance of coming out of this relatively unscathed.

'Not a bit,' she declared. 'I'm willing to listen to her side with an open mind. I'm also certain there's a reasonable, logical explanation for whatever happened, although I can't believe the hospital fired her a year ago. Where has she been in the meantime?'

Noah didn't feel it was his place to tell her, especially since the exact details were still hazy to him.

'In any case,' Harriet maintained, 'Herb has probably blown a minor incident out of proportion and I'll bet my next social security check on it.'

Noah hoped Harriet was right. Sadly, a grain of truth usually rested at the heart of every rumor. The most difficult challenge lay in sifting through the accompanying chaff.

'The future of the pharmacy is at stake here,' Harriet continued. 'If folks refuse to buy from her, she can't stay in business. I, for one, hate to see her hard work and fresh ideas going down the tubes.'

So would I, Noah thought. Holding up her end of the promise to Earl hadn't been easy, and he wanted her to succeed. Not because he wanted a pharmacy in town—which he did—but because he'd begun to sense how important the store had become to her. In fact, his buttons were near to bursting with pride over her accomplishments. Some might say he'd taken a paternal interest in her, but he knew his feelings for her were definitely not of a familial nature. He'd slay dragons for her if he could and now he had a golden opportunity to do so.

Harriet barely paused to draw breath. 'You'll check into this, won't you? And stop Herb's story?'

'I'll try,' he said, his gut feeling warning him that the task wouldn't be as easy as Harriet thought. 'It's after four. I'll catch her before she leaves work.'

The creases of strain in Harriet's face lessened. 'I'm glad you're going to straighten it out. If I can do anything on her behalf...'

'I'll let you know.' He escorted her to the door. 'Now, don't worry. It'll all work out.'

He checked the batteries in his pager and called an early end to his day before he drove to the drug store. Once he'd heard Jenny's version, he'd think of a way to squelch Herb and Twyla's mean-spiritedness before they completely ruined Jenny's reputation. As Harriet had said, a blow like this could easily spell financial disaster.


Jenny walked around the room, straightening the merchandise into nice tidy rows. The products on the lower shelves—the perfect height for young children—rarely remained in their proper positions by day's end.

She paused by her summer products display, pleased by its success. She'd sold a lot of suntan lotion, including the sunless tanning *crème* in the last few days. Adding the toys as props had been a stroke of marketing genius. Children had stopped to finger the shovels and buckets, and while anxious mothers had steered them away those same women had often added a tube of sunblock to their purchases.

By the time she'd replenished and rearranged her goods, the heavy back door slammed.

'Anyone home?' Noah called.

'Right here,' Jenny answered, pleased and puzzled to see him. 'I thought you weren't coming over until later.'

'I wasn't. Something came up.'

The gravity on his face sent an apprehensive shiver

skipping down her spine. 'What's wrong? Is it Carrie? Oh, my God,' she whispered prayerfully, covering her mouth with both hands. 'I told her she was supposed to call me if she had a problem.'

Distraught, she elbowed a first-aid kit into her neat rows of antibiotic ointments and set off a chain reaction that didn't end until every tube had toppled over.

He grabbed her by the elbows. 'It's not Carrie.'

She stared up at him, unable to imagine what could possibly have caused his serious expression. 'Then what?'

'Maybe you should sit down.'

Too shell-shocked to notice his hands guiding her to a seat, she vaguely heard the familiar creak as she lowered herself onto one of the straight-backed chairs in the waiting area.

'Harriet came to me just a little bit ago,' he began, settling on the chair next to her. 'Herb's telling tales.'

'About my uncle?'

He hesitated. 'No. You.'

Her mental warning system began to sound an alarm. 'Me?'

'Yeah. His story is that you left your hospital job in Grand Junction under suspicious circumstances. A patient died because of pharmacy error.'

For a few moments she didn't move. How had Herb got wind of that horrible time in her life? The period that was best forgotten? Noah's guilty expression suggested that he'd only recapped the story's highlights.

'Is it true?' he demanded.

Jenny had hoped the ghosts of her past would have remained in the shadows where they belonged. She should have known better. 'Part of it.' She stood. 'I've got to go home. It's nearly five and Carrie will be worried.'

He grabbed her arm as she took her first step. 'Dammit, Jenny. Talk to me. Which part is true?'

'Does it matter?' she asked quietly, seeing frustration and curiosity reflected in his eyes.

Noah paused. 'Not to me. But to everyone else in town? Yes, it does. This news has shaken their confidence. They don't like to think of anyone in the medical profession making an error. They forget we're human.'

She nodded. That particular mindset had fueled many malpractice suits. 'It's not as melodramatic a picture as Herb has painted.'

'Don't you think it's time to tell me what happened?' His gaze latched onto her with an unshakeable intensity.

Sensing his expectant mood, she sank back into her chair and braced herself to begin.

'I started working in the pharmacy right after I got my degree. I loved the hustle and bustle of the hospital, and when my uncle asked for me to join him I decided against it.'

'So you stayed in Grand Junction.'

'Yeah. Things were fine for a while—I loved my job— until the hospital ran into budget problems. After exceeding their allocations for both the first and second quarters of their fiscal year, Administration froze our vacant positions. To maintain our shift coverage, we worked longer hours. Basically, we did more with less.'

'Unfortunately, health care is heading in that direction,' he said.

'Our frequency of errors increased. It was inevitable, considering our workloads had nearly doubled. We had a system of checks and balances, but as time went on there were more and more instances of nurses on the floor catching our mistakes. Things like the wrong dosage, sometimes even the wrong pill.

'The department head ignored our complaints. He'd found greener pastures, so he didn't really care. Shortly after he left, they promoted one of the senior pharmacists. We were sure things would change because Ted had worked in the trenches and knew the pressures we faced.

'Unfortunately, he turned his back on us. He only wanted to please *his* boss, not concern himself with the low morale of his staff. We tried to appeal to him, to remind him of what life was *really* like, but we got counseling memos and bad evaluations for our efforts.' She paused. 'Do you know what happens when you continually mention problems that the supervisor wants to overlook?'

'I have a good idea.'

'Anyway, I'd dated Ted on occasion, so my colleagues thought I'd have better luck appealing to his common sense.'

'Did you?'

'Hardly. He listened to what I had to say, then offered me the shift supervisor position I'd hoped to earn some day. In exchange, he expected me to support his decision to trim more of the "fat" from the department.

'I refused and Ted accused me of not being a team player.' She shuddered, remembering his cold-hearted smile as he'd reminded her of the tie between her job performance review and future pay raises.

'What happened next?' His voice was low.

'It all came to a head one evening. I was working alone, and had prepared a heparin solution for a new patient. As you know, the dosage and rate of infusion is dependent on the weight of the person.' He nodded and she inhaled a bracing breath before she continued.

'I made my calculations for a one-hundred-ninety-pound woman and told the nurses on the floor how fast to run the heparin in her IV. Unfortunately, the patient was a *ninety*-pound female—the squiggle that I'd read as a one was just a stray pen mark—and the rate I'd calculated was much too high. The nurse started the infusion per my instructions and, luckily, she mentioned what she'd done in passing to one of her colleagues. The other nurse realized it wasn't right and immediately stopped the IV. If she hadn't, the patient could have died.'

'But she didn't.'

'No, but the possibility was there. Ted landed on me with both feet. His incident report stated that I was inattentive to detail and he recommended disciplinary action. After that, he found fault with everything I did and I completely lost my confidence. I probably shouldn't have, but the culmination of everything was more than I could take. So I walked away and started over as a substitute teacher. Later, I was offered a full-time contract of my own.'

'You could have come home. Earl would have understood.'

'I know, but I couldn't face him. I only wanted to forget it ever happened. I knew Uncle Earl dreamt of me joining him, but staying away was easier than shattering his hopes.'

'Yeah, but you're here now and that's what matters. As for Herb, the truth will be our defense.'

The way he included himself caught her by surprise. Before she could comment, he fired another question.

'How does Twyla fit into this?'

'Mrs Beach is one of my aunt's cronies. My aunt would dearly love to see me fail and obviously Twyla is willing to help her cause.'

'But why is Twyla saying you gave her the wrong medication?'

'I changed suppliers and the diuretic she takes came

from a different company. The pills don't look the same, which is why she says I gave her the wrong medication. I explained it all to her at the time and thought she understood.'

'Then we'll just have to set people straight. With Harriet and myself behind you, Herb's rumor won't go far. We'll start by—'

'No.' She shook her head for emphasis.

'No?'

'This isn't your problem to fix.'

'Well, now,' he drawled, 'I happen to think it is.'

She glared at him. 'How do you figure that?'

'It's simple. If Herb manages to drive your customers away, you can't stay in business. If you aren't in business, I'm back to my original problem of not having a local pharmacy for my patients.'

'Oh.' So much for thinking that his recent attentiveness had been in *her*—he'd only been interested in her professional skills. Instantly, she berated herself for forgetting two important things. One, he'd clearly have walked through fire to ensure the town had its blasted drug store and, two, he abhorred the notion of appearing before an altar.

'So, in the meantime, act normal.'

'But I did something wrong. You can't deny it.'

'You made a mistake,' he corrected. 'Yes, it could have been tragic, but it wasn't. Even if it had been, forgive yourself and chalk it up to a learning experience. If you dwell on the past, you'll miss out on the future.'

'Right now, the future doesn't look too bright.' Contrary to whatever means Noah had in mind to stop Herb, she could only see one way to effectively silence the man.

Another pharmacist must take her place. If she left the picture, Herb's attempt to destroy her business would fail.

In the end, everyone would have what they wanted. Noah would have his local drug store and she would have…her students.

Although she enjoyed teaching, the thrill of being in teenagers' company didn't compare to being in Noah's. But what did she expect? While she liked her kids, she was astonished to discover she'd fallen in love with Noah. Until she proved to him that she *could* keep her promises—namely the one to her uncle—her romantic chances with the handsome doctor were slim to none. If leaving sooner than she'd anticipated advanced her cause, she would endure the next nine lonely months of school with the proverbial smile on her face.

'I think the future looks very promising,' he declared. 'And don't you forget it.'

She answered him with a smile, choosing not to mention her strategy in the war with Herb. Everything hinged on finding a suitable replacement for herself, so until that happened she wouldn't say a word.

He rose. 'Why don't you lock up and go home? Carrie's probably wondering where you are. I'll swing by after I pick up a pizza and the ice cream.'

'I thought you were busy this evening.'

'Only until eight,' he said. 'It's nothing that can't be changed. The guys can get along without me.'

'Don't be ridiculous. Carrie and I can occupy ourselves for the next few hours.'

He cupped her face in his hands. 'I'd rather eat pizza with you than play basketball with a bunch of over-the-hill men.'

'Are you saying that you're over the hill?'

Noah grinned. 'I'm still in the prime of my youth.' He pressed his lips against hers in a brief but spark-filled kiss.

Prime condition was an apt description. Her toes curled

in her sandals as he tasted her mouth with the ardor of a man savoring a delicacy. She dreamily wondered how many times she could manage to travel from Grand Junction to Springwater during the next school year.

Jenny would simply pin her hopes on the adage, 'Absence makes the heart grow fonder.'

'I'll be at your house in about forty-five minutes,' he said, pulling away. 'After we eat we'll put our heads together and figure out the reason for Herb's vendetta.'

If he could focus on the situation at hand, so could she. Before she could explain Herb's motives, as she knew them, Noah had left. She quickly straightened the merchandise she'd knocked over, locked away the petty cash and bolted the doors.

Shortly after Jenny came home to a sunburnt but bored Carrie, Noah arrived with a large half pepperoni, half hamburger pizza, a carton of vanilla ice cream, and a two-liter bottle of root beer. He'd also exchanged his heather-green twill trousers and matching polo shirt for a pair of gray athletic shorts and plain T-shirt.

'When are we going to set up for the sidewalk sale? It's tomorrow, you know,' Carrie said as they sat down at the kitchen table.

Jenny slid a slice of pizza onto a plate. 'I brought the boxes out of the basement and stacked them by the front door. In the morning, we'll carry out our tables and you can arrange everything just the way you want it.'

For the rest of their meal they discussed the best sales strategies, and Carrie talked of all the things she would buy with the money she earned.

Jenny hoped she wouldn't be disappointed.

After they'd cleared away their dirty dishes the phone rang as if on cue. Suspecting that Susan was making her weekly phone call, Jenny sent Carrie to the extension in her uncle's den. Ten minutes later, Carrie returned.

'Mom wants to talk to you,' she said.

Jenny picked up the wall-phone's receiver. 'Are you tired of roughing it yet?'

Susan moaned. 'You can't imagine how tired I am. But good news. I should wrap things up in a week. I'll drive out for Carrie on the Saturday after the holiday.'

'So soon?'

'Yeah. I guess you could say that Mother Nature's been co-operative. We stayed on schedule.'

'I'm glad for your sake, but I'll miss your daughter. She's been a great help. I never thought I'd say this, but I'll even miss Bugs.'

'Yeah, the furball does grow on you,' Susan admitted before her tone became teasing. 'I hear you're entertaining company. *Handsome* company. Maybe I should pick Carrie up earlier. I'd hate for her to put a damper on your love life.'

Jenny's skin heated at the sly note in her friend's voice. If Susan only knew how one-sided the romance actually was.

Aware of Noah sitting nearby, she turned her back and chose her words carefully. 'She isn't. Besides, I need her.'

'Ah,' Susan said, knowingly. 'You need a buffer.'

'Maybe.' Her answer was telling in itself. In her thirty-two years, she hadn't met anyone before who had challenged her restraint like Noah did. With his kisses packing so much punch, Carrie's presence had kept her from throwing her morals out the window.

Then again, Noah had never asked her to discard her principles. Either he'd opted against pursuing that avenue or he was simply biding his time.

Hoping for the latter, a shiver coursed down her spine.

'Something tells me there's more to it than that, but I'll leave it alone for now,' Susan said. 'When I get there, though, I want details. Every last one.'

'Fair enough.'

Noah smiled at her as she sat down again. 'Everything all right?'

She nodded. 'Susan's coming for Carrie next Saturday. This weekend will be our last one together. I'll have to plan something special.'

'A carnival's coming to town. Maybe she'd like to go.'

Jenny beamed at him. 'Perfect. She loves those.'

With that decided and Carrie ensconced in the living room, watching an old Lucille Ball episode, Jenny watched Noah adjust his glasses. The motion seemed a signal to open the subject she'd been dreading.

'The best defense is a good offense,' he began.

Inwardly she groaned. 'I'll warn you right away. I have a mental block where football is concerned.'

He grinned. 'It's OK. I'm trying to make a point. We can spend our time trying to defend you, or we can take the offensive.'

'You mean, dig up some dirt on Herb and spread it around.'

'Not exactly. If we can figure out Herb's motives, we can turn the information to our advantage.'

'I know his motive. He's angry because Earl didn't leave the pharmacy to him.'

'Should he have? I mean, was Herb a long-time employee?'

Jenny thought a moment. 'He came three years ago. Four at the most.'

'Could there have been a verbal contract between him and your uncle?'

'It's possible, but I doubt it. Herb would have said something right away and he didn't.'

'Good point.'

'My uncle was very protective of his livelihood,' Jenny explained. 'He could have taken a partner at different times, but he always refused.' She paused. 'You two were good friends—did he ever mention anything to you about changing his will?'

He shook his head. 'Not even a hint.'

Carrie's giggle drifted in from the other room. Jenny chuckled at her enthusiasm.

'She's enjoying herself,' he said.

'Oh my, yes. She loves *I Love Lucy* reruns.'

Noah slid his fingers underneath his glasses and rubbed his eyes. 'Why do I feel like we're missing something?'

'I don't know what it would be. He probably thinks that if he can't own the store, neither should I.'

'Did he plan a buy-out? Either from Earl when he retired, or from you?'

She shrugged. 'It's possible, I suppose. But, again, he never mentioned it. In fact, he didn't even make me an offer. Believe me, I would have considered one.'

He seemed incredulous. 'Were you that anxious to dump the store on someone else?'

'Yes, but not for the reasons you suspect. After dealing with my aunt for a month, I wanted to sever all ties between us. She was just as eager to see the money from the sale and her attitude was the sooner, the better.'

'So she sold her half to you.'

'Between my savings and a hefty loan, I managed to scrape up the funds. Tom Rigby pulled quite a few strings for the bank officials to grant my application.'

Once again he fell silent, as if mulling over possibilities. 'Herb resigned, right?'

'Absolutely.'

'Since then, did he ever indicate that he regretted his action? Maybe he wanted to come back.'

'Then he had a funny way of showing it,' she said, dismissing the theory outright. 'When he came into the store the other day, he seemed surprised at all the changes. I'm sure he thought I couldn't manage without him and was shocked to see how well I had.'

Noah leaned closer, his gaze intent. 'What did he say to you?'

She hesitated, trying to remember. 'He asked about a box of personal income-tax papers that he'd stored in the basement.' Anticipating Noah's next question, she added, 'He went downstairs to get them, but returned empty-handed. I told him that I'd keep my eyes open and let him know when I found his files.'

'Was he satisfied with your answer?'

'I thought so. He offered to help me look through the boxes whenever we decided to clean out the basement, but I didn't commit myself one way or another. At the time, it seemed a nice gesture on his part.'

'So why would he switch from being kind and courteous to spreading malicious rumors?'

'What can I say?' She shrugged. 'He has a screw loose.'

Carrie walked into the room. 'What does that mean?'

'He has a screw loose?' Jenny asked. Carrie nodded and Jenny clarified, 'It means he has a mental problem.'

'Oh. I thought you were talking about real screws in people. One of my friends' moms had screws put in her ankle.'

'Doctors sometimes use them to hold people's bones together while they heal,' Jenny said. 'My comment was a figure of speech.'

'Oh.'

Noah's eyes took on a thoughtful gleam. 'Maybe...'

Jenny jumped to her feet, guessing what had torn Carrie away from her program. Besides, their discussion should wait until they had one fewer member in the audience. 'We've hashed this over long enough. How about a root beer float?'

'I was hoping you'd say it was time,' Carrie said happily.

Jenny ruffled her hair. 'Want to help?'

Carrie nodded, then faced Noah. 'Do you wanna help, too?'

He rose. 'Sure, sprout. What do you want me to do?'

'You can get the glasses from the china cupboard in the dining room,' Jenny directed. 'They're on the top shelf. Carrie will show you.'

Carrie and Noah disappeared into the other room while Jenny dug her ice-cream scoop out of the silverware drawer and pulled the carton out of the freezer.

'We found 'em,' Carrie declared as she led the way into the kitchen, carrying one of the three tall, crystal parfait glasses. 'They're kind of dusty, though.'

Jenny squirted dish soap into the sink and turned on the tap. 'That's easily fixed,' she said. 'The teatowel is hanging on the oven handle.'

'Hinting for me to dry?' Noah asked.

Jenny looked at Carrie. 'He's such a smart man, isn't he?'

Carrie giggled.

As soon as the glasses were clean, Jenny scooped ice cream while Noah poured the soda until the foam rose high above the rim. 'And now for the crowning touch,' Jenny said, opening the refrigerator to retrieve a small jar. 'Maraschino cherries.'

'Can we eat outside?' Carrie asked. 'Bugs would like the company.'

'As long as you don't drop your glass on the concrete,' Jenny cautioned.

'Is it 'cause these are 'loons?' Carrie asked, studying her drink.

Puzzled, Jenny glanced at Noah. 'Loons?'

His eyes took on a teasing glint. 'Yeah, Jenny. You know about loons, more commonly known as heirloons.' He winked.

'Yeah, that's it,' Carrie said. 'So where's the bird?'

Jenny laughed. 'The word is heirloom,' she said, emphasizing the 'm' sound. 'They're personal family possessions that get saved and passed on to descendants. These particular glasses belonged to my grandparents.'

Carrie listened wide-eyed as she slurped the foam off the top. 'I guess they're yours now.'

'I guess so,' Jenny said slowly, realizing the frightening responsibility she'd inherited.

But later, as they sat outside on the porch steps in what seemed like domestic bliss, Jenny wondered about the next generation of Ruscoes, and if there would even *be* another generation.

Why couldn't Noah be someone who trusted in forever-after promises?

The next day—Thursday—keeping his promise to Carrie, Noah arrived bright and early to carry the tables and boxes of saleable junk outside for the annual sidewalk sale. Carrie insisted on organizing everything herself so, after casting a benevolent smile upon her, he left.

Throughout the morning Carrie conducted a booming business while Jenny struggled to occupy her time. She filled the hours with odd jobs and busy-work, carefully watching Carrie wheel and deal with prospective buyers for her merchandise.

Although the people who stopped to purchase the odd assortment of gifts, games and other sundry items were friendly, Jenny sensed a wariness in their attitudes.

Don't be paranoid, she told herself, forcing herself to act as if she hadn't noticed the change. As for her own lack of customers, she blamed her decreased sales volume on the sidewalk sale. Shoppers were nosing out bargains, not necessities like aspirin and corn-removers.

After lunch, Carrie started her 'two-fer' special, which meant customers could purchase two items for the price of one. Children popped out of the woodwork to buy the knick-knacks, intent on purchasing the best for themselves.

'I hope you consider a career in sales,' Jenny said at the end of the day. She'd been pleasantly surprised to see how well Carrie had done, both in terms of money earned and merchandise sold. Even board games with missing pieces had been purchased after she'd parceled them into packages of replacement parts.

'You've got to convince people you have something they want,' Carrie said importantly. 'The rest is easy.'

How sad to be taught marketing concepts by a child.

'Miranda's lemonade stand did real well, too,' Carrie commented. 'Can I set one up next week?'

'Don't expect to earn as much as she did,' Jenny cautioned. 'You won't have the crowds we saw today.'

Carrie pursed her lips together in thought. 'That's OK. I'll think of something to draw people to my stand.'

Jenny smiled, wondering what Susan would say when she heard about her daughter's exploits. 'All right.'

Carrie's smile grew wide and she hurried to the phone to share her good news with Miranda.

*     *     *

Friday morning brought in two customers. A teenager who played tennis purchased an elbow wrap and Rodney Meder bought a box of insulin syringes.

The afternoon dragged by, and as Jenny locked the doors for the night, she excused the day's decreased sales on people not being in a buying mood.

Her theory sounded lame even to her own ears.

That evening, Noah obviously saw through her fake cheerful front. 'Not a good day?' he commiserated.

'No.'

'I usually hear the rumors flying around town, but no one has said anything to me.'

'Do you expect them to?' she asked. 'Everyone's aware of how much time you're spending with me. They're probably afraid to broach the subject.'

'I'm sure everyone has already dismissed the gossip.'

'Could be,' she said noncommittally, unable to ignore her lack of customers but not wanting to dwell on the situation. Her applicants would arrive on Tuesday, after the July Fourth holiday, and then she'd implement her own plan to salvage the Ruscoe business's reputation.

'What are you doing this weekend?' he asked.

'I'm sifting through Earl's things in the house.'

He frowned. 'I'm booked for an overnight fishing trip—the guys planned this months ago—but I can cancel.'

'Don't be silly. Carrie and I will manage on our own.'

He studied her for a long moment. 'Are you sure?'

She smiled. 'Of course. How hard is it to pack things in boxes and give them away?' Actually, the task wouldn't be easy. These were Earl's possessions, the items he had used or saved for posterity. Things like an old pocket watch, photographs of long-dead ancestors, and a quilt her grandmother had made. They deserved her time and reverence as she decided their fate.

'You can join us, though, when we go to the carnival on Sunday evening.'

'Great. I'll be here.'

Although Jenny and Carrie spent the weekend inspecting the nooks and crannies of the house, Jenny realized how time dragged without Noah. Even the box of old papers and ledgers she'd removed from the pie safe didn't capture or hold her interest.

Get used to it, she scolded herself as she shoved the box back in the closet where she'd originally placed it. He won't be in Grand Junction.

As the hours drew closer to their date for the carnival, her spirits rose. Although she normally avoided the stomach-dropping, head-twirling rides, she actually enjoyed them with Noah at her side. The teddy bears he won at the ring toss—one for her and one for Carrie—touched her. The stuffed animal with its lopsided smile earned the status of a prized possession.

Picnics and fireworks filled Monday. Each event, each moment spent with Noah, entered a special place in her memory, to be removed at some later date and savored once again.

All too soon the realities of life intruded. Tuesday morning brought an increase to her business traffic, but not to its previous levels. By lunchtime she'd sold a few items of little consequence and decided that Carrie had proved herself capable of handling the cash register while she conducted her interviews.

After Jenny had dutifully admired Carrie's sign for her lemonade stand and tasted the tart drink she had prepared, the first job applicant arrived.

John Bellamy was a quiet man in his early fifties, had

never married, and liked the idea of having a nearby lake in order to pursue his boating and fishing interests. Although he was personable and willing to follow Jenny's direction, he seemed more focused on his hobbies than on providing ideas to attract new clientele.

Zoe Doran was a vibrant redhead in her mid-twenties, who professed to love challenges and was excited over continuing the plans Jenny had outlined. She even made a few suggestions that Jenny thought had merit.

Her enthusiasm reflected the very traits Jenny wanted in the future manager of Ruscoe Pharmacy. Although Ms Doran seemed somewhat vague about her reasons for re-locating to Springwater and, in fact, seemed almost desperate for the job, Jenny didn't press for answers. Zoe went on to promise a minimum one-year commitment, which reassured Jenny. Zoe wouldn't be here today and gone tomorrow.

Jenny discussed the salary she could afford to pay, but Zoe didn't bat an eye at the bad news. Taking her stoic acceptance of those conditions as a good sign, Jenny didn't waste any time making an offer.

'The job's yours, if you want it.'

Zoe's face lit up. 'I do. When do you want me to start?'

'Whenever you can.'

'I'll have to find a place to stay…'

'If you're interested, you can live in my unc—*my* house, rent-free,' Jenny said, willing to compensate for the lower income in this manner. 'That is, if you don't mind sharing with me when I come to town.'

'Not at all,' Zoe said. 'I'll be here next week.'

'Perfect. We'll have about a month to work together and learn the ropes before school starts.'

After working out a few other minor details, Zoe left with a definite spring to her step and a smile on her face.

Jenny watched her leave, satisfied that everything was working according to plan. Her gaze landed on her uncle's blue coat hanging behind the door. Hiring Zoe was in the pharmacy's best interests, she thought.

She knew all of this in her head, but not in her heart. The prospect of leaving her store in someone else's hands—even if they were capable—pained her far more than she'd dreamt it would.

# CHAPTER TEN

JENNY reminded herself of the facts. Her options were limited and this was the solution. The *only* solution to her current problems.

The sight of Twyla Beach coming into the store seemed like a horror of fate. Too bad Zoe wasn't available to deal with this woman. Carrie couldn't, which meant the task fell to Jenny. However, before she could rescue Carrie, Twyla marched up to the eleven-year-old.

'Is Jennifer in?' Twyla demanded.

'She's back there,' Carrie said, pointing toward the prescription area.

Jenny stepped into her line of vision. 'Good afternoon, Mrs Beach,' she greeted her politely from behind her counter. 'How are those pills working for you?'

The sour expression on the older woman's face matched Eunice's perfectly. 'Fine,' she said shortly. 'I only came in to tell you what I've heard.'

Jenny stiffened. The sudden sly look in Twyla's eyes worried her, although she pretended indifference. 'Oh?'

'I just came from the Chamber of Commerce. My neighbor is their secretary and she told me the most interesting tidbit.' She paused in an obvious attempt at drama.

'A new drug store is coming to Springwater.'

Jenny's smile froze. The town could barely support one, much less two. 'Competition is always nice.'

'Yes, but that's not all,' Twyla added triumphantly. 'Dr Kimball invited them to town.'

This time Jenny couldn't disguise her surprise. 'He did?'

'Oh, my, yes.' Twyla waved a hand airily, although her gaze remained sharp. 'Apparently Dr Kimball contacted the corporate office and suggested they look into opening a branch here. In fact, he's meeting with them this afternoon.'

Jenny swallowed hard and hid her clenched fists in the pockets of her smock. She'd never imagined he'd do such a thing to her and her mind reeled under the weight of the information.

'It's rather shocking since you two have gotten so, shall we say, chummy? Then again, maybe he knows something that the rest of us don't.'

Jenny's anger rose at the innuendo. 'As one of the town's doctors, he obviously does or he'd be spending his day spreading rumors like certain other small-minded people in this town.'

Twyla gasped. 'Small-minded? Are you implying…?'

'If the shoe fits…'

Twyla blinked like an owl before she raised her nose in the air and sniffed. 'Well, I'm not going to stand here and listen to this.'

'No,' Jenny said evenly. 'You probably shouldn't.' She might regret her outspokenness later, but right now it felt satisfying to give the Twylas of the world a dose of their own medicine. 'Have a nice day,' she added in dismissal.

Twyla stomped from the building, slamming the door hard enough to rattle the window.

Shaken by the whole encounter, Jenny retreated to her makeshift office. Noah had invited a business rival to town? The idea seemed far-fetched, considering how much he'd helped her, and yet it made perfect sense. He would do whatever he could to achieve his own goals.

Apparently, he doubted her ability to weather the latest setback to her business and had taken matters into his own hands.

The traitor.

When would she learn that men looked after their own interests? Well, it was high time she did the same.

She began filing away Zoe's and John's résumés for safekeeping, hating to see the tremor in her hands as she stuffed the papers into her employment file.

Contrary to what she'd told Twyla about competition being a good thing, in Springwater it spelled doom. Two pharmacies couldn't survive, especially when a large chain store boasted distinct advantages over those of private ownership. She couldn't benefit from their ability to purchase large quantities at a discount, then turn around to pass the savings onto the consumer. Naturally, consumers patronized those places where they could buy their necessities at a lower price, and eventually small businesses like hers withered and died.

Once again the death knell of Ruscoe Pharmacy seemed to sound in her ears. She sank onto a chair and mulled over her next move. None came to mind. Her stomach churned at the idea of bringing Zoe into this mess. Hopefully, she could contact her and rescind her offer before Zoe resigned her present job.

Frustrated tears burned in her eyes and she quickly brushed them away. She wanted to march over to Noah's office and give him a piece of her mind. Surely he was finished meeting with his new cronies.

'I'm sorry, he's not in this afternoon,' Tanya apologized after Jenny telephoned his office. 'He'll call in for his messages before long, so I'll ask him to get back to you.'

'Don't bother. I'm sure I'll see him later.' Jenny broke

the connection. A few hours' delay wouldn't make a difference. Time wouldn't diminish the anger—and hurt—burning inside her.

'Jenny?' Carrie's small voice sounded tentative.

Jenny looked toward the half-door and saw Carrie's face framed in the opening. 'Yes, honey?'

'Are you OK?'

Jenny cleared her throat. 'Yeah, sure.' Her words carried a husky quality and she swallowed hard. 'Why do you ask?'

'I heard what that lady said. Why did Noah invite another pharmacy to move into town?'

She sighed. 'I don't know, dear. I wish I did.'

'I thought he liked our store.'

*So did I.* 'I don't know what he thinks,' Jenny answered honestly. 'But it doesn't matter. We won't give up yet. Just because another company is considering opening a branch here, it doesn't mean they will.'

'Then we don't need to worry 'cause they can change their minds?'

Jenny nodded, forcing herself into optimism. 'Absolutely.'

'I'm glad. Maybe if Noah tells 'em that we don't need 'em after all…'

How ironic to hear Carrie express her faith in the man who'd caused this disaster. 'It doesn't work that way. The company will make their own decision.'

'Are you mad at him?'

'Furious' described her feelings more accurately, but she watered them down for Carrie's sake. 'Let's just say he's not on my list of favorite people at the moment.'

Carrie nodded, her expression knowing. 'That's what my mom says when she's mad at someone.'

Jenny managed a smile at the little girl's insight. 'I guess I am.'

'My mom says it's healthy to let yourself be angry, as long as you don't let it last for ever. You aren't going to stay mad at him for a long time, are you?'

'I don't know, Carrie. I just don't know.'

But she did know. Her anger would last until the hurt faded. She stopped a moment to consider why his actions had caused such pain and realized the reason a split second later.

She loved him.

Now was certainly a fine time to figure *that* out, she thought crossly, wishing she could turn those feelings off. Sadly enough, she couldn't.

'Oh.' Carrie seemed to consider Jenny's comment before she spoke again. 'Miranda and I have our lemonade stand set up outside. Is it OK if we start selling our drinks now?'

It took Jenny a few minutes to register the shift in conversation. 'Yeah, sure,' she said, glad to see Carrie would have a friend to keep her company while Jenny reconsidered her plans for the future.

'I'm going to keep Bugs with me.'

'Watch out for Mr Henderson's Dobermann,' she cautioned, hating the idea that the rabbit might become an entré. Although the furniture store owner kept Chester in his store, and swore the pet was well-behaved, who knew what would happen if he caught the scent of fresh prey?

Carrie nodded. 'I will. I'll keep Bugs on his leash the whole time. If he starts acting funny, I'll bring him back inside.'

Noah slid out of his Blazer and smiled at the children gathered around a card table in front of the drug store.

One girl, who was close to Carrie's age, held Bugs in her arms while two others jostled each other to be next.

'How's business?' he asked, noticing that the sign's message included the opportunity to hold Bugs with every purchase of lemonade.

'Pretty good,' Carrie said, before she glanced at her watch. 'Time's up,' she announced. 'Who's next?'

'Me!' another youngster piped up as she plunked down her quarter. Ignoring the cup Miranda had placed on the card table, she held out her arms and waited for Carrie to hand Bugs into her care.

Obviously, Carrie had decided to capitalize on Bugs's appeal to sell her drinks. From the half-full cups lining the table, the kids preferred holding the rabbit to wetting their whistles.

'Is Jenny inside?' he asked.

Carrie nodded. 'Yeah, but I wouldn't go in there if I were you.'

His hope of telling Jenny about her potential competition before she heard it elsewhere died. 'Then she's heard?'

She motioned him to the side, away from the small crowd. 'Yup. Mrs Beach told her this afternoon.'

He was too late.

Noah rubbed the back of his neck and heartily wished Twyla Beach would suffer a severe case of laryngitis, one that would be incurable for at least several months.

'No siree. Jenny's not happy with you.' She planted her hands on her hips. 'Neither am I.'

If the situation hadn't been so grave, he would have been amused by Carrie's expression. Unfortunately, the situation *was* serious and all he could do was explain, cross his fingers and hope for the best.

'Don't you like *our* store?' she asked.

'I do,' he said.

'Then tell the other people not to come,' Carrie demanded.

'I'm afraid it's not that simple,' he said gently, wishing it could be otherwise.

'I thought you were our friend, but you were just pretending, weren't you?'

'No,' he insisted. 'I wasn't pretending.'

Carrie rolled her eyes. 'Yeah right. Jenny's in her office. At least she was earlier. If she doesn't talk to you, don't say I didn't warn you.' She walked away to rejoin the group surrounding Bugs.

Squaring his shoulders and steeling himself for a tense encounter, Noah entered the store. If not for a radio supplying background noise, he would have thought the place deserted.

Jenny appeared at the prescription counter's window. Her welcoming smile disappeared. 'Oh. It's you.'

Her flat tone bothered him and he tried to break the ice. 'I see Carrie's found a way to attract a crowd.'

'At least one of us is successful.'

'Look…' He moved in closer, aware of how she kept the barrier of the counter between them. 'I came to explain.'

She held up her hands and shook her head. 'Don't bother. I'm not ready to listen. Later I might be, but for right now I *want* to be angry.'

'I can understand that, but let—'

'You hurt me, Noah.'

Her quiet tone worried him more than if she'd ranted and raved. 'I didn't mean to. I'm sorry.'

'You let me think we were in this together—us against them. Instead, you had so little faith in me you switched sides for the one guaranteed to come out on top.'

'No. That's not how it happened.'

'In the end,' she continued, ignoring his protests, 'the town would have its pharmacy and you would be hailed as a hero.'

A muscle worked along his jaw. He suspected he'd be several inches shorter by the time she was through venting her anger.

She gestured in the air to caption a headline. 'KIMBALL NAMED CITIZEN OF THE YEAR. SAVES CITY FROM LOSS OF—'

'That's it,' he said, grimly advancing toward the half-door and throwing it open. 'Enough is enough.' She backed up until she hit the edge of her desk.

He leaned over her, nose to nose. 'You may not believe me right now, but I'm going to explain and you're going to listen. Then, if you want to tear more strips off my hide, go ahead.'

Noticing her precarious balance, he placed his hands on her shoulders and gently pressed downward until she had no choice but to sit on top of the desk or topple over into his arms.

She sat. Several pieces of paper fluttered to the floor, but he ignored them.

'None of this is what you think.'

She raised one eyebrow but, as if sensing his mood, wisely kept silent. Instead, a mulish light came into her eyes and she set her jaw in inflexible lines.

'I'm sorry about inviting Prescriptions Plus to check out the potential in Springwater. I called them right after you announced you were going out of business. They never got in touch with me and I thought they weren't interested. The very next week I learned that you had decided to stay and I completely forgot about them.'

The stubborn tilt to her chin softened and the fire in her gaze fizzled out by slow degrees.

'It's true,' he insisted. 'You can ask Della.'

For a long moment she didn't say anything. Noah watched her intently, waiting for a sign of some sort to indicate that she understood.

'I admit the whole thing looks and sounds suspicious from your point of view. Fault me for being impatient and taking matters into my own hands, but not for anything else.'

'And what am I supposed to do now? You met with the competition. Are they coming?'

'They haven't decided yet,' he said honestly, hating the position he'd placed her in. 'They prefer to locate in larger towns, but admitted they saw an opportunity here.'

'That's some consolation, I suppose.' She met his gaze. 'So why *did* you come around and help me? Were you only keeping tabs on us?'

'I wanted you to succeed.' He hoped she'd accept his simple explanation. 'At first, I wanted it because of what your business meant to the town, and for what Ruscoe Pharmacy had meant to Earl. Later, I wanted it because of you.'

'Fine,' she snapped. 'Then I expect you to give the same attention to my employee after I'm gone.'

'Employee?'

She raised her chin. 'I hired my replacement today. Ms Doran's starting next week.'

He couldn't believe she'd made her decision so quickly. 'Next week? Why so soon?'

'Because she's free and it's high time that I went back to where I belong.'

'You belong here.'

She blinked, clearly startled by his vehemence. 'Do I?'

'Of course you do!' he exploded. 'Why wouldn't you?'

Before she could reply, Miranda dashed into the store, wailing as if she'd suffered a mortal injury.

Jenny jumped to her feet, the bitter taste of fear in her mouth. 'What's wrong?' she asked, pushing her way past Noah to join the girl.

'Bugs ran away. Carrie says you have to help us find him,' she sobbed, tugging on Jenny's hand to pull her toward the door.

'What happened?' Noah asked.

Miranda sniffled. 'We were busy watching out for Mr Henderson's dog so we didn't notice Mr Kravitz and his St Bernard coming from the other way. Baron started barking and Bugs jumped out of Ashley's arms. Before Carrie could grab his leash, he was gone.'

'Where's the dog?' Jenny asked, afraid to hear that Herb's pet had chased after Bugs and was presently making mincemeat of him.

'Mr Kravitz took Baron home to calm down.'

Jenny glanced down both sides of the street. 'Where's Carrie?'

Miranda pointed to the right. 'She and the other girls went over there.'

'Let's fan out,' Noah said. 'He can't have gone far.'

Jenny rounded the corner, conscious of Noah matching her strides. Carrie stood a block away, calling out Bugs's name in a voice laced with tears, while her friends combed the bushes along the sidewalk.

As soon as Jenny caught up to her, Carrie flung herself into her arms. 'Oh, Jenny,' she cried. 'I can't find Bugs and I looked everywhere.'

Jenny hugged her, hating to think of how Carrie would cope if Bugs had disappeared for good. 'Are you sure he came this far?'

'I saw him run past this building.' Carrie motioned to the discount store a few feet away. 'Then I didn't see where he went.'

'We'll find him,' Noah promised.

Jenny privately warned him not to make any promises he couldn't keep. As if he'd understood her unspoken message, he matched her gaze with a steady one of his own.

Carrie wiped her eyes and rubbed her nose with the back of her hand. 'He's dragging his leash. He could choke to death if it catches on something. And what if he gets stuck some place and a dog decides to eat him?'

'Let's think positive,' Jenny said, cringing at the picture Carrie had painted.

'Rabbits are good at hiding,' Noah said. 'He's probably found a nice shady spot and he's waiting for you to take him home.'

Carrie's expression grew hopeful. 'Do you think so?'

'Absolutely,' he said firmly. 'Now, rather than all of us looking in the same areas, we'll split up so we can cover more ground.'

His take-charge attitude and self-confidence visibly restored Carrie's hope. Determination replaced the fear on her cherubic face and she shouted for her friends to join her.

'You've restored her faith in you rather quickly,' Jenny remarked in a tone meant for his ears only.

He shrugged. 'It appears so.'

'Don't let her down.'

'I'll do my best not to.' He paused. 'I'll do my best for you, too. You can count on it.'

She cast a dubious glance in his direction, but let the subject drop. The four girls had gathered around Noah like children around the Pied Piper and were chattering away like a group of blue jays.

'OK, girls. Listen up. Here's what we're going to do,' he began. 'Pair up and we'll search the block. If Bugs is hiding under a bush or in a hole, we should see the leash. We'll stay in sight of each other, and if anyone spies him don't move and don't try to pick him up. One of you signal for Carrie so she can get him. He's scared and won't run away from her.'

All the girls nodded, their faces shining with purpose as he sent them on their mission.

'I'm going back to the store to lock up for the night,' Jenny told him. 'I'll join you after I'm finished.'

'OK.' Noah and Carrie started forward while Jenny backtracked to their starting point.

She quickly hauled Carrie's lemonade stand and her two chairs inside, and turned the front door's deadbolt behind her. Later, after Bugs had been found, she would return to fold the card table, wash out the insulated Thermos of lemonade, and store everything away. Neatness took a distant second to finding Bugs.

Jenny rushed through the building to the rear exit. Just as she reached for the knob, she heard a thump outside. Could Bugs have found his way back?

She flung open the door and instant relief swamped her. Seeing the black and white rabbit waiting on the step like an invited guest, she wanted to shout for joy.

'Why, Bugs, you rascal,' she said, crouching down to scoop him into her arms. 'Did you decide you'd had enough excitement?'

Bugs nuzzled his nose in her elbow as she scratched his ears. 'You deserve a treat for coming home by yourself,' Jenny crooned. But as she turned to go inside something in her peripheral vision caught her attention.

She stopped to slowly scan the area until she realized what was odd. The small basement window was open.

How had that happened? Jenny hadn't been in the basement for days. Carrie had gone down this morning in search of cardboard for her sign, but she wasn't tall enough to reach the latch, or strong enough to push the window open.

Determined to close it, she hurried inside and headed for the lower level.

A strange, albeit familiar smell greeted her at the top of the stairs. Flicking on the light switch, she slowly descended the steps.

Oddly enough, the smell grew stronger until she recognized it. Charcoal starter fluid.

How had *that* got downstairs? More importantly, how had it spilled?

As Jenny stepped off the staircase to walk around and survey the area, she couldn't believe what lay before her eyes. Formerly stacked boxes were now scattered across the room with their contents strewn across the floor. Wet splotches covered everything and the lighter fluid fumes permeated the air. A pile of wet newspaper lay in one corner.

Fear prickled at her nape. Bugs's ears pricked up and his body tensed in her arms as if he, too, sensed the danger in the air. Suddenly eager to call for help, she turned toward the stairs and froze.

Herb Kravitz stood on the bottom step, a box of matches in his beefy hand. 'You had to quit looking for the rabbit, didn't you?' he accused.

'You did this?' She shook her head. 'Of course you did. Why?'

'I can't find my books and I don't intend for anyone else to find them either.'

'You're willing to burn the place down for your income-tax papers?' Suddenly, everything fell into perfect order. 'Those weren't income tax papers, were they?'

He scoffed. 'Not hardly.'

'Ledgers?' she guessed.

'Among other things.'

'You took the missing medicine,' she said in wonderment as the truth dawned. 'What did you do with everything? Sell it?'

'You're not going to be around to repeat my story, so it won't hurt to tell you,' he boasted. 'You're right. I sold every vial and every tablet—my own little business on the side. I ordered extra stock and let Earl pay the bill. Then, after the products had sat on the shelf for a while, I hawked them at reduced prices to a select group of customers who wanted to pay less.'

'Pocketing all the money for yourself.'

His grin was feral. 'Yeah. It worked great. Of course, I didn't turn a profit if my family needed something.'

'How generous,' she said sarcastically.

'Oh, but I was. For instance, take my nephew. A few months ago, his registered quarterhorse had a corneal abrasion. After doctoring it for weeks, the vet finally discovered it was caused by a fungus. My nephew couldn't afford to treat the animal with fluconazole and other antibiotics for six to eight weeks at roughly eight hundred and fifty dollars a week, so I helped him out. Nice of me, wasn't it?'

No wonder the finances of the pharmacy had been in such terrible shape. 'I thought Uncle Earl took care of the ordering and paperwork.'

'I lied. We both did.'

She frowned. 'The handwriting wasn't much different.'

'Practice makes perfect, although I never did get it quite right.'

To think he'd accused her uncle of drinking in order to account for the difference. Righteous indignation flared, but she knew she had to remain calm.

'Why did you quit if you had such a great system in place?' she asked. 'I wasn't around most of the time. You could have got away with it for years.'

'You were digging into the records. I didn't know how much Earl had told you or what you'd found. After years of trying to earn my family's respect, I wasn't about to take on a prison record. I thought if I left you'd close and no one would ever know.'

'But I didn't close.' If not for Noah, Herb could have got away with his misdeeds. 'Why didn't you just take the evidence?'

'I have most of it, except for one ledger which I couldn't find. Earl threatened to go to the police, so I knew he had stashed my book somewhere for safekeeping. It wasn't in his house—I checked after his accident— so it had to be in this building.'

'You had plenty of time to search,' she said, thinking of the month after Earl's accident when Herb was basically alone.

He motioned around the room. 'There are fifty years' worth of paper stored down here. I'll bet every invoice and every ledger your family ever put their hands on is somewhere in this room. It wouldn't take much for Earl to hide my records in the clutter.'

Her relatives' propensity for being packrats had been either a blessing or a curse. After she got out of this, she would figure out which it was.

'Once you came to town, you hung around so late that I couldn't get in and look. Still, I managed on a few nights. I had almost finished searching the basement when you changed the locks. The pie safe and a few cartons were all I had left to go through.'

She thought back to the morning he'd dropped in. 'No wonder you looked so surprised when you saw I'd restored the pie safe.'

'Yeah. So then I had to start searching all over again. I decided not to waste any more time, so here we are.'

She thought of the box in the closet of Earl's study. Thank God Herb didn't know she'd moved those documents elsewhere.

And thank God that Carrie was searching for Bugs with Noah, instead of being trapped here with her.

# CHAPTER ELEVEN

'IT's time for me to leave.' Herb struck a match against the side of the box, then threw it onto a pile of soaked newspaper about four feet away. With a whoosh, the fluid ignited instantly. The edges of the papers blackened and curled, sending up a dark plume of smoke.

Bugs's nose twitched and his hind legs dug into Jenny's abdomen as he tried to escape her hold. She wasn't about to let him go. She'd never find him again.

Herb repeated the process, this time throwing the match in the opposite direction before he climbed three stairs. Jenny watched in horror as flames licked at a cardboard box.

Tendrils of smoke filled the room and tickled her nose, but she didn't let go of the rabbit. 'You killed Uncle Earl, didn't you?'

He stopped and faced her. 'His brakes failed. What a shame, too. That's what happens when a person doesn't maintain his vehicle.'

Her eyes began to water and she coughed. 'You won't get away with this.'

'Sure I will. This whole building is a fire hazard. Everyone knows the wiring is faulty.'

Flames crackled around her. Sweat beaded on her skin, formed by fear and the rising room temperature.

'Gib replaced every last strand. Carrie and Noah both know we don't have any flammable liquids down here. You'll be the prime suspect.'

'I'm going to be long gone. Actually, you brought this

on yourself. If you'd closed the business in the first place, this could have been avoided.'

She coughed as her lungs started to feel the effects of the smoke. 'I'm not responsible for your life of crime, so don't blame me for your poor decisions.'

His chuckle was eerie and reminded her of something out of a horror movie. 'Yeah, well, I'm not the one who's going to be part of a barbecue.'

He backed up several more stairs, his features blurred by the smoke filling the room. 'Enjoy your final moments.'

Desperate times called for desperate measures. 'Don't be too sure of that. You'll have to get past Noah.'

As he turned to look, she loosened her hold on Bugs. Guided by his instincts to escape the danger, the rabbit jumped onto Herb in his rush to reach safety.

Caught off guard by six pounds of energy in motion, Herb toppled over the railing and landed on the concrete to lie motionless on the floor. Carried along by Herb's falling momentum, Bugs landed feet first on the cement. The loop of his leash caught on a broken piece of the wooden handrail and prevented his escape.

'OK, Bugs. I've got you.' Jenny freed the nervous rabbit, staying clear of his powerful hind feet until she'd grabbed him by his nape and tucked him against her. Knowing she couldn't help Herb by herself, she hurried up the stairs, out of the smoke-filled basement and toward the nearest phone.


'Where could he be?' A worried Carrie slid her hand into Noah's as they searched another block for the elusive pet. Everyone else had gone home and only Carrie and Noah continued their quest for the missing rabbit.

'He's around somewhere,' Noah said, trying not to let

his own concern show. Not only had he expected to find the bunny before now, but an hour had passed since he'd seen Jenny. An uneasy feeling had started to unfold inside him and he didn't know if it was on Bugs's behalf or on Jenny's. 'Let's head back. Maybe Bugs found his way back to the pharmacy by himself.'

'OK.'

As soon as they rounded the corner to their block, Noah sniffed the air. 'Smells like someone's burning their supper.'

'I don't think I can eat until I find Bugs. My stomach won't let me.'

He tried to tease a smile to her face. 'Not even pizza?' She shook her head.

As he approached the alley behind Jenny's building, Noah's apprehension grew. The smell in the air was growing stronger and more unpleasant.

'Stay here,' he commanded Carrie before he jogged into the graveled parking area where Jenny always parked her car. Immediately, he saw black smoke curl out of the small basement window. Fear for Jenny bloomed instantly. Nothing could happen to her—he wouldn't let it. And if it had... He quickly forced those thoughts out of his head. The idea of losing her was more than he could bear.

'Call 911,' he shouted to Carrie. The little girl's face turned white and she scampered off without argument.

Noah felt the back door and knob. Both were cool, so he pushed his way inside.

'Jenny?' he called, anxious to hear her voice.

She coughed. 'I'm here. In the office.'

He met her and grabbed her by the shoulders, aware of Bugs in her arms. Relief at seeing her in one piece poured through him and he was torn between hugging her close and scolding her for remaining in a burning building. He settled on a quick hug—the rebuke would come later. 'We've got to call the fire department,' he said.

'Already have.'

'Then let's go.'

She stopped. 'Can't. Herb's down there.'

'In the basement?'

'He started it. I'd be down there instead of him if not for Bugs. But we have to get him out. Not much time.'

He made an instant decision. Knowing the town only had a volunteer firefighting force, they couldn't waste the precious moments they had.

'Do you have a fire extinguisher?'

She nodded.

'Get it. I'll take care of Bugs.' As soon as she handed him over, he hurried outside to tie the rabbit's leash to Jenny's car door handle. By the time he returned, Jenny had a fire extinguisher in her hand.

'Stay here,' he ordered, taking it from her. From the way she was coughing, she'd already inhaled enough smoke.

She shook her head. 'He's too heavy for you. You'll need me.'

'I can handle it.'

'It's *my* building. *My* business. *My* fault.'

He shook his head. 'Stay here,' he repeated, this time with more force. He turned away to test the door leading to the basement. It felt warm, but not hot. Holding his extinguisher at the ready, he cautiously began his descent.

'He's on the floor to the right of the staircase,' she said in his ear. 'The fire's mainly along the right wall, by the window.'

Before Noah could castigate her for following him, he stumbled over Herb's feet. Jenny grabbed the extinguisher and sent bursts of chemical foam onto the closest flames. While she bought them a few minutes of relative protection, Noah examined the man responsible for their predicament.

He found a knot on Herb's head the size of a goose egg, and a foot twisted at an unnatural angle. However, breathing presented more of an issue than anything else.

Jenny crouched beside Noah. 'Extinguisher's empty. Not much time.'

He stifled his own cough. 'Get him on my shoulders.'

As Jenny helped Noah position Herb in a fireman's carry, Noah ignored the moan of pain slipping out of Herb's mouth. It couldn't be helped under the circumstances and, if the truth were known, Noah didn't feel much sympathy toward the fellow.

Two fireman, dressed in full firefighting gear with oxygen tanks strapped to their backs, met them at the stairs where they immediately took over.

Noah willingly surrendered his load to them, then grabbed Jenny at the waist to propel her outside into the fresh air and sunshine. He wouldn't breathe easily until he knew she was well away from any threat.

Before he could reach the ambulance waiting at the street near the rear of the building, a loud whoosh and a small explosion rocked the structure. The fiery beast had clearly found a new supply to feast upon.

Noah pushed Jenny underneath him as they dove to the ground behind her car. More fire trucks and police cars arrived on the scene, turning the chaos into organized pandemonium.

'Noah! Jenny!' Carrie's scream floated over the sound of breaking glass and roaring flames.

Not waiting for Jenny to find her own footing, Noah picked her up and hurried her to the far end of the parking lot where Carrie stood next to a policeman and the ambulance, clutching Bugs in her arms.

'Are you OK?' he asked Jenny, not caring that the EMTs could hear the frantic worry in his voice as they worked on Herb. He ran his gaze and his hands over her body, noting the small cut over one eye and her scraped knees.

She coughed. 'Fine.'

Ignoring his own aching lungs, he plucked an oxygen mask out of an EMT's hand and placed it over her nose and mouth before he accepted one for himself.

Unable to see clearly through his smoke-coated lenses, he tucked one stem of his glasses in the front opening of his shirt. His vision clear in the bright sunlight, he watched Jenny's labored breathing ease and hugged her in relief.

Minutes later, he listened in stunned horror as she related her story to the waiting policeman. If Herb hadn't already been unconscious, Noah would have enjoyed punching his lights out.

Later, after the ambulance had left for the hospital, he stayed with Jenny and observed her carefully for signs of shock. To his surprise, tears streamed down her face, leaving sooty trails underneath the clear plastic mask.

She waved in the direction of her burning building. 'Fire. All gone.'

He understood her message. 'Nothing, I repeat *nothing*, in that building is as important as you are. I don't know what I would have done if you hadn't come out of there when you did.'

She appeared startled by his vehement statement. 'Really?' she croaked in wonderment.

'Yeah. What were you thinking of when you followed me down there?' he bellowed.

'Someone had to watch your back.'

Even though he recognized the truth in her statement, he wasn't finished airing his worries. 'I should shake you for doing something so foolish.'

A smile tugged at her mouth. 'You are.'

He froze, realizing that he was, indeed, shaking her. Grinning sheepishly, he hugged her once again.

Of all the challenges he'd faced, the thought of losing Jenny because of a misguided sense of responsibility was too frightening to contemplate. Even more frightening was the thought of losing her to someone else when he wanted to be the one she turned to in times of trouble.

To think he'd compared her to Patricia, imagining her unwilling to honor her responsibilities, unable to keep her commitments. Jenny had literally stuck with him through the fires of hell, to watch over him like a guardian angel.

The last of his doubts and fears disintegrated. He couldn't let a woman like her go.

Twenty-four hours later, Jenny gazed upon what was left of Ruscoe Pharmacy. Everything in the basement was a total loss. The floor in her office had fallen through, destroying her entire pharmaceutical inventory. The goods near the main entrance of the store had been damaged by the heat, the smoke, and the water. Her antique furniture could be salvaged, but only with a great deal of effort.

All of her dreams, her desires, her plans for the future had literally gone up in smoke. Promise or not, fate had conspired against her. She couldn't recover from this setback and didn't intend to try.

As she peeked through the main entrance she was conscious of Noah's comforting presence. He'd hardly left her alone since last night, except for a few hours early this morning. Although she'd encouraged him to go about his own business he'd hung around anyway.

'How's Bugs doing?' Noah asked.

'Great. Rabbit treats are on me for the rest of his days.' She owed that ball of fur a debt she could never repay. Without him, she might easily not be standing where she was today. A cold chill enveloped her, in spite of the ninety-degree temperature, and she rubbed at the goose-bumps on her arms.

'Herb's going to the county jail as soon as he leaves the hospital,' Noah mentioned. 'Along with his customers. The police are also looking into the possible tampering with Earl's car.'

The loose ends were finally being tied. 'I'm glad.'

'What are you going to do now?' he asked, motioning to the structure in front of them.

Jenny managed a smile. 'Rent a bulldozer?'

His gaze was intent through his glasses. 'Seriously. What are you going to do?'

She stared at the smoke-blackened walls. 'I am serious. I know when I'm beaten.'

Noah hesitated. 'I was hoping you'd want to start over.'

'I think the smoke addled your brain instead of mine. There's no way I can afford to and I certainly don't have the desire. I've done it too many times already. I can't do it again.' I'm sorry for letting you down, Uncle Earl.

'Maybe not by yourself…'

'That reminds me. I've got to get in touch with Zoe,' she said, thinking aloud. 'Unfortunately, her phone number is a small pile of ashes. I guess I could call Directory Assistance.'

'Before you do that, why don't you consider taking on an investor?'

Jenny narrowed her eyes. 'I won't bring anything to a business partnership. It's all gone.'

'No, it's not. You can contribute yourself.'

'In other words, I'll be an employee.'

'Not if the arrangement is something along the lines of what's mine is yours.'

She stopped in her tracks, unable to believe what he was saying and unwilling to raise her own hopes. 'What are you saying?'

'I don't want you to leave Springwater. Or, if you do, I want to make sure you'll come back.'

'Why?'

'Because you'll take a part of me with you wherever you go. I want my ring on your finger so you won't forget that there's a man in Springwater who promises to love and cherish you.'

She'd wanted to hear that for so long. Now that she had, she could hardly believe it. 'You do?'

He nodded.

'And you're asking me to marry you?'

He acted amazed. 'What did you think I was doing?'

Her spirits rose out of the ashes of her former despair. 'I just wanted to make sure we were both on the same wavelength.'

'We are.'

'I distinctly remember you saying that you weren't planning on getting married.'

'That was then. This is now.' He paused. 'I can't ask you to risk everything again if I'm not willing to do the same.'

His statement touched her, but she faced a more pressing problem. 'But what about Prescriptions Plus? I can't afford to compete—'

'I spoke with them this morning. They're willing to let

you buy their franchise. You can take advantage of their name and all the benefits associated with being part of a chain and still retain ownership to do things your own way.'

His solution seemed too good to be true. 'Really?'

He nodded, his eyes twinkling. 'Yes, really.'

'But what about—?'

'We can deal with the details later. If you're willing, that is.'

The hope she hadn't wanted to experience refused to be denied. 'I'm willing, but are *you* sure?'

He hugged her close. 'If you ask me that one more time, I'm going to resort to drastic measures.'

She couldn't resist being coy. 'Which are?'

'I'll farm Carrie out to Mary Beth's for the night and show you,' he murmured.

She practically melted in his embrace. 'So we can have a wedding? The church, bridesmaids, flower girls, the whole nine yards?'

Panic flitted across his face before stoicism appeared. 'If that's what you want.'

'I'll compromise,' she said, imagining a small informal garden affair instead of the large, formal ceremony he dreaded and the elopement he preferred. 'But I still have to finish out my contract with the school district.'

'Can I talk you into breaking it?'

She pretended to be horrified, although she was secretly pleased at the wistful note in his voice. 'Go back on my word? For a man who values keeping one's promises, how could you think such a thing?'

Noah bent his head to brush his lips against hers. 'It's fairly easy,' he said. 'When I think of what waiting is going to cost me.'

'It's only nine months.'

'Yeah, but we could have our first child by then.'

'Actually, I'd like to have you to myself for a while,' she said softly, fingering the placket of his shirt.

'Then you shall,' he said, bending his head to press his mouth against hers.

His kiss sent a tingle down to her toes. The Ruscoe Family era hadn't ended—it was just beginning.

# MILLS & BOON®

*Makes any time special*™

## Mills & Boon publish 29 new titles every month. Select from...

Modern Romance™          Tender Romance™

Sensual Romance™

Medical Romance™  Historical Romance™

MAT2

# FREE!

## 4 Books

### and a surprise gift!

We would like to take this opportunity to thank you for reading this Mills & Boon® book by offering you the chance to take FOUR more specially selected titles from the Medical Romance™ series absolutely FREE! We're also making this offer to introduce you to the benefits of the Reader Service™—

- ★ FREE home delivery
- ★ FREE gifts and competitions
- ★ FREE monthly Newsletter
- ★ Books available before they're in the shops
- ★ Exclusive Reader Service discounts

Accepting these FREE books and gift places you under no obligation to buy; you may cancel at any time, even after receiving your free shipment. Simply complete your details below and return the entire page to the address below. *You don't even need a stamp!*

**YES!** Please send me 4 free Medical Romance books and a surprise gift. I understand that unless you hear from me, I will receive 6 superb new titles every month for just £2.40 each, postage and packing free. I am under no obligation to purchase any books and may cancel my subscription at any time. The free books and gift will be mine to keep in any case.

MOZEB

Ms/Mrs/Miss/Mr ...................................................Initials..................................

BLOCK CAPITALS PLEASE

Surname...........................................................................................................

Address.............................................................................................................

.........................................................................................................................

......................................................................Postcode ..................................

**Send this whole page to:**
**UK: The Reader Service, FREEPOST CN81, Croydon, CR9 3WZ**
**EIRE: The Reader Service, PO Box 4546, Kilcock, County Kildare (stamp required)**

Offer not valid to current Reader Service subscribers to this series. We reserve the right to refuse an application and applicants must be aged 18 years or over. Only one application per household. Terms and prices subject to change without notice. Offer expires 28th February 2001. As a result of this application, you may receive further offers from Harlequin Mills & Boon Limited and other carefully selected companies. If you would prefer not to share in this opportunity please write to The Data Manager at the address above.

Mills & Boon® is a registered trademark owned by Harlequin Mills & Boon Limited.
Medical Romance™ is being used as a trademark.